MATCH

FIT

Love and Play Series

BAD BOYS AND
SHOW GIRLS

AMÉLIE S. DUNCAN

Published by Amélie S. Duncan
Copyright © Amélie S. Duncan, 2017

ISBN-13: 978-1539603764

Cover Design by Sommer Stein of Perfect Pear Creative
Main cover model image licensed from (and copyright remains with) Wander Aguiar Photography
Formatting Design by Champagne Formats

Some British slang words and grammar included in the story

MATCH FIT

CHAPTER

ONE

Brooke

could see the headlines starting with, *"Famous Retired Financial Guru Allister Starling's Daughter, Brooke, Bottoms Out at the Bargain Bin."* The salesperson's barely disguised glee at my misfortune grated on my nerves, as I frantically searched through my purse for a different card to pay for a new pair of Converse Chucks. I was sure I had an extra seventy dollars sitting in my account after paying off my bills.

Knowing I now had an overdraft charge because of a pair of fifty-percent-off sneakers got to me. I not only bankrupted myself over a pair of cheap shoes, but I disgraced the family name by melting down over it. Taking place on a poorly planned shopping spree among the after-work crowd in Times Square, on my twenty-third birthday, no less.

While I'd imagine the press enjoying my shame, he'd

recommend that I return to Seattle and "get real," his slogan for a "needlessly" struggling artist like myself. "If you haven't gotten a steady acting job after two years, then it's time to find a stable career." One that could afford to pay all the extra upkeep, such as the photo shoots for composite cards, dance and acting lessons, and the all-day auditions. I vowed I'd make it on my own, and I would do it. Even if it meant embarrassing myself at a shoe store. I've been ashamed before. I would double my efforts to earn more or cut back a dance class. Whatever it took to pay the overdraft and fix my bank account.

Lifting my chin, I took my cheap shoes and my scratched-up debit card from the saleslady's outstretched hand and moved aside to begin my inevitable walk of shame. Turning on the heel of my old pair of scuffed-up pink Chucks, I walked by the row of stink-eyes from impatient shoppers to the sidewalk in front of the shop. The chilly, damp wind had me putting on my raincoat. Summer weather was often unpredictable.

Leaning against the glass front of the building, I stared out at the neon lights of Broadway like a tourist enamored with the city for the first time. The people crowding the square—singers, dancers, power suits, families, and every nationality all in one exciting and thrilling soup of possibility—reminded me why I had chosen to come here in the first place. The place thrived on opportunity. While I hadn't seen my name in lights yet, I had a chance to try. I had possibility.

My ringtone was set too loud and it cut through the noise of the people passing by me on the sidewalk. It was my alarm. I was late for work. I took out a tissue and wiped away any tear streaks. Meltdowns were, as my mother would put it, a private thing. One mustn't ever make a scene.

My job as a singing and dancing waitress at Colby's Truck Stop required a happy disposition. It was a well-polished, modern-day Western saloon, with sawdust on the floor, carved four-top tables with barrel chairs, and two walls of barrel-ended booths. In the center was a small curtained stage for us cowgirls to sing and dance before the upright piano. Sure, the Daisy Duke rip-off outfits of short-shorts, red plunging neckline gingham crop tops, and sparkly cowboy boots were a little degrading. And don't get me started on the blonde pigtail wig I had to wear over my dark red hair. But the country music had grown on me. It was a gimmicky tourist trap, but I enjoyed it.

Colby's was the one job I had where I could perform in public five nights a week. Five chances for an agent or casting director to see me and enable me to get my big break. My dad would call that one of my "rose colored dreams." But I was one degree away from it happening. In fact, it had happened to my best friend and roommate, Gemma, last month. After singing Carrie Underwood's "Jesus Take the Wheel" one night, she got a call from our agent, Raymond Walker, about her performance. One thing led to another and boom! She landed the part of factory worker number four in the Broadway musical *Les Misérables!* Who knows? Today could be my day.

With a renewed sense of purpose, I put on my backpack and surged forward in a zig-zag pattern through the maze of people, across the square to the front of the line at the door of Colby's. Frieda, the hostess, was glaring at a pushy tourist and his family, who were impatiently waiting for seats as she checked her chart. When her eyes flicked to me trying to scoot by, I gave her one of my silly renditions of a panting puppy dog that made her laugh. We all worked to brighten up the tense moments.

Once inside, I hurried past the row of booths to the back of the office to change into my uniform. I had half of my clothes off, standing by the metal lockers, before I registered the manager, Sandra, which was pronounced "Saundrah," standing at the end in the doorway. She always stood out among the country kitsch dressed in one of her suits. "You're ten minutes late," she said when I finally made eye contact.

I dropped my gaze. "Sorry. I had an audition." Auditioning was the one excuse we all were allowed to use once a month, and I hadn't used mine yet. It was a little lie. I had one yesterday, thanks to Raymond.

She softened a touch. "That's great news. How did it go?"

I shrugged. Truthfully, it hadn't gone anywhere. Raymond said they were looking for mysterious, sexy women. He of course failed to tell me they were looking for Asian mysterious, sexy women who could pull off a convincing line in Mandarin. Still, I made it through the first cut, not bad for a five-foot-eight freckled redhead. Bottom line, I didn't get it, but I wouldn't tell Sandra that. After all, if there was one thing I learned in this business, it was that no one likes whiners. So I told her a little lie. "I think it went well. Thanks."

I slipped on my uniform and my eyebrows lifted. She

was still standing there. "Something else on your mind?" I asked.

"My sister Brenda's coming back."

I tucked my hair under my wig. Brenda had left when I started here five months ago. Although we only over-lapped a day or two, she had come by with her adorable newborn baby boy for visits. "How is Josh?"

She blinked. "Oh. Josh is fine. He's in daycare. And, well, actually, that is the reason I came back to see you. Since Kevin's hours were cut at his job, she needs to come back to work to pay for daycare. We'll cut back hours to help accommodate the change. You're not fired."

I smeared my gloss. The dreaded F-word. "That's good," I said slowly.

"But since you were our last hire, I must cut your hours to alternate weekends on the morning shift."

My stomach knotted. Alternate. "Two days every oth-er week in the morning?"

She nodded. "A temporary layoff, but with the sum-mer, I will more than likely call you to cover shifts."

"Oh," was all I could muster. Those hours were as good as being fired. From twenty days a month to four on the shift with the worst tips. I wouldn't be able to pay my half of the rent. A wave of nausea rose up within me. My one steady job, gone.

"Well, things change every day. Who knows? I may be begging you to come back," she said with a dry laugh.

I giggled a little. "Well, you know I love working here and thank you for the opportunity."

"Hey!" she said and lightly tugged on one pigtail. "You're still on the books and at the top of the list to call if the situation changes."

I plastered on a smile. *No guarantees.* "Thanks! I'd better get out there."

"Yes. Great," she said with a lift in her tone. I could almost see the bubble next to her head that read, "That went better than expected." She turned at the doorjamb and said, "Uhm…happy birthday."

I swallowed hard. Losing jobs in a harshly competitive market was a good cause for a meltdown. Once again, that was not something I'd do in public.

I took the quick hug she gave me. And I did one of my silly twirls that made her laugh before returning to the restaurant. As that old song went, "When you feel like crying, make them laugh."

I didn't have time to moan. And with a check of my uniform, I made it out the door in time to join the group at the front doing the country line dance number to Trace Adkins' "Honky Tonk Badonkadonk." Hey, not my favorite Trace Adkins song, but we didn't get to choose. I knew the dance moves, though, and sprang into action. I went up to the small raised platform stage and took my spot between Tasha and Yasmin. We did the tit and ass gyrations and twerks along with the line steps that we saved for the evening. I was in the zone. I didn't miss a beat.

The crowd got into it with catcalls. For the most part we didn't mind. The performance was great for tips.

Afterward, I cleaned up, snagged my faux-wood electronic pad and readied myself to take orders at the tables.

"Brooke. Can I switch tables with you?" Tasha asked, sliding into the space next to me at the pickup counter.

My brows lifted. "Why? Did something happen?"

We all got difficult tables from time to time. And I was poised to give her a pep talk and change with her when she shook her head and motioned toward the corner booth in my section where two men were seated. The blond had wavy hair pulled back in a fashionable man-bun. A printed, sleeveless T-shirt molded to his lean, yet muscular chest. His tan, sinewy arms were on full display, showing off gorgeously crafted tattoos from shoulder to bicep. He was gorgeous, without a doubt, but there was something about him that was familiar. Just then, as if on cue, the blond's head turned our way and as I saw his stunning profile, recognition hit me.

"Dylan Pierce and Knox Callaghan from F.C.!" she squealed.

Sure enough, it was Dylan Pierce. The new player for the New York City Football (Soccer) Club had come to Colby's. He was the big transplant from England's Manchester City Premier League. His face and incredible physique were plastered everywhere lately. From photos with the team to modeling designer underwear, he had been on every billboard and subway platform for months.

I glanced at the man seated across from him. Knox had short wavy black hair and was just as yummy, with sleeve tattoos and tiny hoop rings in his ears. He was posing and grinning like a crazy cat as some of our star-struck patrons snapped away at them with their phones.

Although I was somewhat familiar with the team, I wasn't a big soccer—or football, as Gemma put it—fan. But I was familiar with Dylan Pierce. Even if he weren't famous, his hot-as-hell looks shone bright. He had what most of us actors would call a million-dollar face. The kind of face made for film. He had the total package: a drool-worthy, muscle-toned body, sexy scruff on his square jawline and full, sensual lips that begged to be kissed.

Dylan was panty-melting hot but, unfortunately, he knew it. That is, according to his bad-boy, tabloid-seeking antics. A few had labeled the pair of them noxious bros, known for booze, broads, and brawls. They had often been photographed dating swimsuit models. And there were plenty of pictures with them groping smiling women. I wasn't one to slut-shame a woman getting hers but, even with some of the raunchier photos being blurred out, you could still make out that their hands were all over the place like they were on some porn shoot and not out in public. I mean, it screamed they didn't care about the women personally, but about what they could get sexually.

Colby's Truck Stop wasn't what I'd imagine as their normal scene. Even so, the city was full of famous people and I knew I could handle their table. Still, I wasn't one to deny a coworker her swoon-worthy five minutes. "Sure. I'll tra—"

But before I could even finish my sentence, a flustered woman approached us, a fussy child squirming on her hip. "Miss Sally?" All of our name tags read "Sally," but since I had only just come on duty, she had to mean Tasha. "Could you please help us with our child's seat?"

Tasha wasn't using her poker face at the moment. She slumped her shoulders and drifted off after the mother and her child without another word, leaving me to go over to Dylan and Knox's table.

I squared my shoulders and strolled on over. They were just customers, but I cringed a little when I had to follow the service script. "Welcome to Colby's Truck Stop. What's your pleasure, sugars?" I drawled out. Cheesy. But going off script could get me fired. Oh, yeah.

My heart pounded as I drew up close to their table. So close that I could see how thick and dark Dylan Pierce's eyelashes were and how they framed his piercing, pale blue eyes. The same eyes that were boldly traveling down from my face to stop at my breasts, making my nipples harden and poke out of the thin fabric of my shirt.

I sucked in air, doing my best not to cover up. But I didn't need to. His eyes quickly shifted to the menu. It was a fast-as-lightning dismissal.

My stomach squelched. What a jerk!

My smile tightened as I shifted to Knox. His eyes were still fixed on my top. His lips quirked up in the corners. "What do you recommend, sweetheart?"

I put a cheerful lilt into my voice as I ran through the specials, all while shrinking inside. Now, I wasn't movie-star hot, but I had been told my face and green eyes were pretty. My nose wasn't a button, but that gave me character. I had, as my mom said, nicely shaped cheek bones and lips. My breasts weren't the basketball size of those women Dylan was normally seen posing with, but they were perky. Whatever. Oh, shit. They were now both staring at my face. Had I pep-talked myself out loud in front of them?

My face warmed. We were all staring until Knox broke the silence.

"We said a couple of burgers," Knox said. "Or should

we wait?" he asked Dylan.

I fought to stay cool while Dylan's stare returned to me and stayed. He took his time before answering him.

"We're not staying long. The others won't eat." His deep, sexy British accent sent a tingle of pleasure through me, which I failed to shut down in its tracks. *He may be insanely attractive, but he's rude.*

I was about to walk away when Dylan said, "You didn't ask about our drinks. I'd like a pint."

"Water for me, sugar," Knox drew out. He was laying it on thick.

I tapped it in and told them, "I'll be back with your orders." And that would have been a clean exit if I hadn't dropped my pad. I bent over to pick it up.

"Bloody hell," Dylan said, and they laughed.

My butt in their face wasn't a clean exit! I tried to right myself and tumbled over. Great! My whole body felt as if it were on fire. As I moved to stand, a warm, strong hand circled my waist.

"You all right, love?" It was Dylan.

I took in a sharp breath and inhaled a healthy dose of his delicious-smelling aftershave. He went from gorgeous to spell-binding up close.

"Thank you. Yeah. I'll be right back."

He was nice, I thought, but then he opened his mouth and said, "Too bad those short-shorts didn't split showing us your honky tonk badonkadonk."

Knox was in stitches now. He added in a few hums of the song for their amusement.

I twisted out of Dylan's grasp and onto my feet. He could go back to ignoring me now.

"Don't get your knickers in a twist, love. It was a compliment," Dylan purred. "You looked like you could use a laugh."

I pursed my lips. Was he serious or was he giving me a pity flirt?! *Screw them.* "Thanks for helping me up, but next time, don't bother," I said with a lot of sass in my tone. "And keep your comments to yourselves. I'll get someone else to bring your drinks."

"Oh, come on, we were joking. Relax," Knox said. "She's wound tight. I wonder how—"

"Leave her alone," Dylan told him.

I didn't wait around to hear the next obnoxious insult. Instead, I marched over to the L-shaped bar before returning to the pickup station for a breather.

I rubbed my neck. Was I overreacting? *Maybe.* I glanced over and saw Dylan was starring over at me. A tingle went through me. I looked away.

"Oh, my God, he touched you," Tasha said dreamily. "I'd drop everything to get a touch," she gushed.

"Hey. You can have them. I'll switch a table with you," I said.

She dropped her mouth open. "Really?"

I handed over my order pad, and we changed the assigned markers. "Yes. Knock yourself out."

She squealed. "You're the best. God. I'm going to miss you."

I sighed. Oh, yeah. I had lost my job. My shoulders drooped as I collected her chicken nuggets child-order and left to deliver it to the table.

I had settled a couple more tables, though my eyes drifted over to Dylan and Knox frequently. They had been joined by a pretty, buxom brunette and an older man in a suit. She was more of the type of woman they usually went for, not that I was interested at all.

The announcement from our piano player cut through my thoughts. "Now welcome our Sally up to the stage to sing Gretchen Wilson's 'I'd Love to Be Your Last.'" That was my cue. I took a deep breath and went back up on stage. I took the microphone, positioned myself in front of the piano and sang.

I had rehearsed the song many times, and I usually gave a good performance, but tonight was different. This performance marked the end of a steady job. The inability to afford a pair of sneakers. And two years struggling in New York City. And what did I have to show for myself? I was in the same place I had been in since I arrived here. Nowhere.

I poured out my soul into that moment. I gave all my yearning and lost feelings to that little corner of the stage in front of an evening crowd in a theme bar. What was I going to do now?

I was alone. Lonely.

I crooned the lyrics that were sweet promises that she'd be there to hold her lover throughout the night and next morning. It wasn't just a song; they were my wishes. Though I wasn't even close to getting them. My chaotic schedule and lack of extra money left me no opportunity to go out and date. Anything beyond that, I was friend-zoned. I was always a friend. But for tonight, this performance, I was more than that. I sang with the passion of a woman who sings this song to her lover. A woman who knew she was loved, special. A keeper.

The eruption of applause around the restaurant brought me back, and I did my cutesy twirl and big smile before leaving the floor, taking in all the well-wishes from all the customers. I couldn't stop myself from glancing toward Dylan Pierce's booth. If I didn't know any better, I'd say he was staring right back at me. Intensely. There came that silly tingle. And there was my heartbeat speeding up like he had done something good. Then again, he could be staring at something embarrassing. Another boob ogle?

I looked down at my chest and sure enough there was more bra showing than shirt. It must have shifted from the twirl. I discreetly fixed it. Knox's now unmistakable hearty laugh filled the area, making me look over at him. Dylan was definitely looking my way. They were thoroughly enjoying picking on me. It usually took a while, but I had already become a source of amusement. Trust me to be turned on by a jerk, as usual! It would have been easy to dissolve and give in to this bad evening, but that wasn't me. I stayed in the experience of my performance. I had sung my heart out, and the crowd responded. That made this a great night.

I went back to work. The time flew by and before I knew it, we performed our finale dance, marking the end of my shift. I was about to walk to the back, when I felt a hand on my arm. I turned and my face lit up. It was Raymond. His tightly curled hair was neatly trimmed, his suit pressed. "Hey, you didn't tell me you were coming here tonight," I teased.

He smiled. "I hadn't planned to. It was a last minute client meeting. Oh, about the audition… Sorry."

I waved my hands. "Next time."

"I just wanted to say you were incredible tonight," he said.

I smiled genuinely. "Thank you."

"Next thing that comes in—" he said.

"You'll call me." I gave him a quick hug and rushed off to the back. Everyone was there, including the kitchen and bar staff. They had gathered around to present me with the farewell apple pie. Mine had a candle shaped in the number "23" sticking out from the middle of it. Everyone broke into a loud rendition of the birthday song.

I bit my lip. This was more final than I had hoped. I blew out the candle and said, "Thank you all," giving hugs all around.

"Oh, here, Brooke," Tasha said. "Dylan told me to give you this. I got one too." It was a fifty-dollar bill.

I shook my head. She had kids. I'd figure it out. "You did the work."

"Nope." Tasha refused and stuffed it in my pocket.

"We're all going to miss you, Brooke. They broke out into the Dixie Chick's "Wide Open Spaces", Colby's Truck Stop's goodbye song.

I sang and danced along. And threw kisses to them on my way out the door. A pause at the exit had me looking back at Dylan's table once more before leaving, to say "thank you." He was no longer with Knox and the brunette. He had been joined by Raymond and an older gentleman. Was Dylan his new client? Raymond was already too big for me, but we got on like friends and that was the main reason he kept me. I'd perish if he even thought to drop me.

I rushed the rest of the way out of the restaurant. I

had made it a couple of blocks before stopping to wipe a tear out of the corner of my eye. It'd be alright. Well, I could always call my parents in Seattle. I turned on my phone and, wouldn't you know, I had a text message from my father.

Allister J. S.: Do you need money again?

I swallowed. Even if I did, I couldn't deal with the "I told you so and you're wasting your life" speech that accompanied it. Nope. I'd find a way. I'd double my efforts to find a job.

Brooke.S:I'm alright, Dad.

I was heading over to the subway when I heard a voice ring out, "Can you spare some change?"

My gaze settled on a woman, her eyes averted, as she sat on a cardboard square. Her dog was yawning at her side with an empty bowl. There were, unfortunately, lots of homeless people in the city. I often tried my best to do what I could with what I had, but something about her made it so I couldn't look away. She started singing, "On Broadway," a song I had heard and sung a million times, and the impact went straight to my heart. This could easily be me.

What you put out could come back to you. I said a prayer and put in the fifty-dollar tip in her hand, wishing I could do more.

"Bless you," she said.

My eyes teared up. "Bless you."

Tightening my coat around me, I made my way down the stairs of the subway, passing a smiling poster of Dylan

Pierce posing in his New York City Football Club, or F.C., attire. He was in a blue and white fitted top and shorts, holding a soccer ball, standing next to a group of kids for the United Nations International Children's Emergency Fund—UNICEF. Oh, he was a handsome devil. I lingered on his full lips that were turned up in a grin. My mind went on to remind me of his generous tips and his work with kids, so he couldn't be all that bad. But then I recalled his and his friend's rude comments in the restaurant and his crass behavior, and I shook my head. I'd take the poster over the real thing any day. With a last glance, I rushed on down the stairs and onto the train.

CHAPTER

TWO

My ride home hadn't improved my day. In fact, the subway train went out of service at Christopher Street, leaving me to walk the rest of the way to our apartment on Avenue C in the East Village. When I got there, our neighbors' tabby cat, Cinder, lured me into a petting session that ended with a bite on my hand. Grrr! Perfect end to the perfect day. I still had my cheap shoes, but I wasn't as keen on putting them on now.

Our building was a bit on the older side, and with echelon stairs and eighties parquet flooring, we had been able to swing the one and a half bedrooms. The half bedroom belonged to me, with a bed from my mom, and a dresser.

After visiting a few of our friends' places, we decided it wasn't too bad. The best features were a faux fireplace and a chandelier. Gemma had brought the shag carpet and black velvet couch with her. We had decorated the walls with free paintings she had gotten from an artist she once dated. My contributions were the easily assembled Ikea chairs, tables, and lamps. We pretty much treated it as a place to sleep, not to hang in. We spent the majority of our time outside of the apartment. Still, it wasn't cheap. When I opened the door, I waved my hands to get the attention of Gemma's shiny boy-toy of the week, Baloo, a hipster with long hair and a beard, and asked him to turn down the music—once he stopped grooving out and registered that I was standing there.

Our landlord was pretty decent and gave us some leeway on the weekends, but I wasn't up for rocking the boat, especially since there was a good possibility that I might be late on rent next month. I was all about lowering my profile.

Gemma strolled in from the galley kitchen with a bottle of wine in hand. She was in her after-show garb of a large sweater and leggings. Her black hair was hanging on her shoulders.

"What happened to the music?" Her deep brown eyes swung my way. She smiled over at me. "Happy birthday, roomie. Alright, Brooke?"

Being from London, Gemma saying "alright" wasn't an opening for me to dump all my woes on her. It was more of the equivalent of the "Hey" greeting here in America. But since I'd earned the beloved titles of "love" and "hon," this now gave me more leeway.

"Colby's is downsizing. Brenda's coming back..." I trailed off, but she got it.

"No way. You're the best singer they have! It's so unfair!"

I grinned. She gave good encouragement. She passed

me the wine, and I took a swig.

"What are you going to do?" Baloo asked.

I squatted next to Gemma on the area rug. "The usual. Hit up all my contacts for work."

"Crystal Ball is looking for burlesque babes," Baloo offered.

I was flattered for half a second that he found me hot enough to think of me that way. "Paid?"

"Not sure," he said.

Gemma frowned at him. She was often impatient if someone didn't have a concrete answer to something they presented before her.

"I'll call," he quickly added.

He looked a little worried that, by intruding in our personal conversation, he now might not get laid. But by Gemma's rules, if he made it inside the apartment, he would get lucky. Then again, Gemma kept her friends and her sex life separate. Therefore, I wasn't surprised when she told him, "Baloo, go on in my bedroom, will you?" Her tone was light enough for him to get up and follow her orders. And even though it held a tinge of snark, she was pretty, which also helped out.

"How was tonight?" I asked her, passing the bottle back.

"Intense. I had to get there early to make sure Julie didn't try to take parts of my costume," she complained. Cattiness ran rampant behind the scenes of the shows because, well, we all wanted to stand out. We all wanted to make it. "So tell me exactly what happened?"

I waved my hand. "Never mind."

"You always do that. I can be a shoulder," she said.

"No, I don't want to go there," I said, hoping to avoid that conversation altogether by changing the subject. "Oh, something else exciting happened. Dylan Pierce and Knox Callaghan were there."

"The footballers?" she asked, shocked. "I didn't think Colby's was their thing—no offense."

At times she forgot she had worked there too. I told her what happened and of my few minutes of shame.

"You stuck your bum in his face?" Gemma mused.

She laughed so hard, tears stung her eyes. In retrospect, it was sort of funny now. I joined in laughing with her. We broke into a sing and dance improv of the musical *A Chorus Line*'s song, "Dance: Ten; Looks: Three (Tits and Ass)."

Once we fell over, laughing, Gemma said, "Really? He sounds like he was making light of it, but given your situation, it's understandable that you were moody."

"I wasn't moody," I said. "The pair of them were being obnoxious."

"Okay. I see you're still bothered. But he did give you a tip to make up for it," she pointed out.

"True," I admitted. And I hadn't even thanked him.

"You could have gone back with him and got your leg over."

I tut-tutted. "And become another number of easy women that would have to do a Hail Mary at the clinic? No thanks."

She laughed. "You're insane. They're hot, I would have gone for it. You are uptight." She switched to her side. "You should give Collin a call. Sex might make you feel better. I know it works for me." She rose, a little unsteady on her feet from hitting the bottle, and passed it back to me.

I sighed. My schedule was chaotic and left no room for relationships. Collin was my stashed-away friend with benefits. He wasn't great in bed, so a climax for me was hit or miss but, God, were his gracious enthusiasm and compliments a total ego boost. "Maybe."

By the time she closed the door to her bedroom, I had already ruled him out. A warm bath and email blast would work just as well.

I drank a little more wine and took it with me into the bathroom where I turned on the bath to heat up the water. While I waited for it to get hot, I sent out a few queries for work.

When I was done with both, I put on my robe and went around the divider to my full-sized bed and sank down on it. The bed was comfortable enough, but so different from my four-poster one in my bedroom back in Redmond, Washington, with my parents. In fact, I could probably fit this whole apartment in my room and still have more to move around. My father had specifically asked the architect to make sure all the bedrooms had a view of Mount Rainier.

My father was a self-made man. He had worked from entry level to the top in corporate banking. He had a killer instinct for the financial market and he invested accordingly, making his fortune.

My mother sold Mary Kay cosmetics and ran a party décor shop in Woodinville. She didn't have to work, but my father wouldn't dream of letting her stay home. He expected everyone to work. And I had through junior high,

high school, and college. The only advice I didn't follow from him was choosing a stable career. He supported hard work and success, not me "finding" myself. While I had asked for money before in tight circumstances, I had, for the most part, learned to do without, and would again.

Before I went to bed, I noticed the light on my phone was flashing. It sometimes went on silent mode. When I checked I found I had a new message from Raymond.

Ray. WTS: Got a job $ Come by tomorrow morning

I quickly called him back. He answered on the first ring.

"Brooke," he drawled out. When he sang my name, it usually meant he had called to discuss a job I wouldn't want to do.

"You called about a job that fits my skill set," I prompted.

"An exciting job," he said. "It's not acting in the traditional sense, but it pays well."

I frowned. "What does it involve?" I couldn't keep the disappointment out of my tone.

He said, "Meet us at eight a.m. at my office tomorrow."

"Wait. Who is 'us'?" I cut in. "You haven't told me what the job involves. Who am I meeting?"

"You, uh, met him already. Dylan Pierce," he said. "Surprise! That's what I was in Colby's for today."

My mouth dropped open. "No way. With him? Doing what?"

Raymond laughed a little. "Well, you know he came over here to be a forward for New York's Football club.

But what you may not know is that he's interested in acting. Something he's looking to take up when he retires."

He paused, as if expecting me to object at the ridiculous idea, but I was too intrigued to interrupt.

"Now, he's had some bumps in publicity with his image. He doesn't want to go the reality route. He wants to be taken seriously. So I presented him with an opportunity to get a more wholesome girlfriend. That's where you come in."

I glared at the phone. Raymond had lost his mind. "You have expanded your services to pimp? He could get an escort for that. Hell, he could get any woman to do that. Can't he get one of his many girlfriends?"

"No, he can't. He's not looking to settle down, and girlfriends don't always play nice. And once he's done, she'll be all too ready to cause more tabloid fodder... Let me explain it another way. Remember Liza Remington? She started dating Samuel Rivers. And now she's on that HBO series. All because she was seen around in public with that star. That could be you with him. He'd have you, a good wholesome woman—"

"Wholesome. Are you calling me ugly on my birthday?" I snorted.

"No. You're pretty and you know it. What I meant when I said wholesome was you're a good girl. You don't do drugs. If you're sleazy, I haven't heard about it, and I talk to everyone. Even if you are, you're an actor, you can pretend not to be. And he can come across as a good guy. Paparazzi snap away and the jobs start rolling in. Everyone's doing it. He gets a chance not to appear too self-absorbed and shallow. This pretend budding relationship would give you a chance to get on the short list for acting roles in theater, TV, and film. What do you say?"

I scrunched my face. "What would I have to do?"

"Go to his games, travel to his 'friendlies', exhibition sports matches, out of state. Be seen taking photos with him. Who knows? If he has scripts, run lines with him. That's it. You'll be the girlfriend experience without the sex," he said.

I licked my lips. Shit, this was sounding alright. And being seen dating an incredibly hot guy like Dylan Pierce wasn't exactly what I'd describe as a hardship. Though this evening he seemed to delight in making me uncomfortable. I bit my lip. "But he doesn't like me. He called me uptight."

"So? Does every actor like who they star with? Let's keep this shit real. You get paid, and free travel with a star athlete," he said. "This could be your big break."

The potential and possibility sounded good. My big break. The core of working show business. Everything was a gamble of potential and possibility. This could lead to being noticed from the crowd and getting a real break, a paid acting job that could jumpstart my career. Being arm-candy for the handsome Brit would definitely get me noticed. He was often in the press.

But on the other hand, not all of his press was good. If he did something scandalous, our fates could be linked with stories that would overshadow any chance at success. He'd probably recover, but what about me? I'd be lucky if I ended up with a reality show offer. Truly, the situation was too risky. My phone beeped, giving me a chance to stall for a bit more time before making a decision. I excused myself and switched lines.

"I got an email alert about the overdraft on your account," my dad grumbled.

"That was my private business, not yours," I said, raising my voice an octave.

"Watch your tone, and it is my business. You're my daughter and you're destroying your life—"

"I'm talking to my agent about a job as an…assistant," I interrupted. "I'll fix the overdraft as soon as I get paid, and that's the last time my bank will be sending any alerts to anyone but me. Talk to you later."

I sighed heavily and took a moment to collect myself. If something went wrong in my life, my father always paid attention. Rarely did he see or comment on the good that went on in my life unless prompted by my mother.

But I didn't have time for that now. Raymond was waiting for an answer and I had the only one I could give him.

I switched back over and said, "Fine. So when do we start?"

"Well, actually, Dylan hasn't completely agreed, but he did agree to meet with us tomorrow morning," he added. "He wants to, but we have to convince him."

"Yeah," I mumbled. *Fuck it.* "How do I need to prepare?"

"Come looking wholesome. Think sweetheart romance."

He had us both laughing at that.

I turned to my computer screen and saw my first rejection email from one of my contacts. I needed this more than not. "Fine. I'll be there."

CHAPTER
THREE

Dylan

The official word was that I chose to come over to the States to join New York City F.C.

I did like the team and the players. But that wasn't the whole story.

I'd had a year or two left in Manchester City. But that wasn't what was happening in the team. The owner had started moaning about some younger guy they wanted in my place. Even after being a big part of bringing the team to the English and Euro Championship. It wasn't enough. My career was done, at twenty-eight years old? Fucking bullocks. There were players still in it. I trained and played harder. I could do it. But it came down to pushing or being pushed. I pushed. I put out the word that I was leaving, and New York F.C. leapt at the chance to take me on.

I left. I decided. I won.

Football was and would always be my game.

Was my stellar career luck? Hell no. I worked my arse off, training in football on a team since I was five. I didn't even stay in the youth academy long before I was picked up by Coventry, and from there I signed professionally. And when I was seventeen, I was part of the senior team on the bench and didn't get used.

It wasn't until the Football Association—FA cup match with a lower league team—that I scored a hat-trick on my debut. The rest got me from Coventry to center forward for Manchester City. I sacrificed everything for it. I lost family. Mates. Women. Training and being the best always came first. And I was the best, *am* the best.

No matter what shite they fill their heads with. It will take more than a season to replace me. I brought the team to championship and lined their pockets. I was a part of maintaining our team. Making our crowds proud to wear our team's kits again. That was what we were talking about at Wallis Agency with Salvatore Rosa, my NY-F.C. "American Liaison and Public Relations Manager," and his pal Raymond, the owner. We were occupying two of the free seats before his desk in a small office on the Upper West Side. Salvatore was busy selling me, as he often did.

"And you will do the same for New York's F.C.," Salvatore said.

"But you need to plan for the long term," Raymond said. "Sports isn't a forever job, like I told you. I'm an ex-footballer. I understand. I had to make the transition. You can and will get better. Trust me, this could work."

Raymond was a nice bloke. I got him. He found a way after it was over that worked for him. His ideas sounded far-fetched but the way he said it sounded good. I still wasn't sure about his girl playing mine.

"Maybe with some other bird," I said. "Yours is too uptight for me."

I let that sink in to the two of them. Raymond looked at Salvatore. My not wanting her was grating on them. They thought she was a sure thing. She was taking this about as seriously as me, but I at least turned up. Hell, it was already after eight, which was the time we had arranged to meet at the office and there was no sign of her.

I knew her name was Brooke Sullivan. Salvatore told it to me yesterday when he got me and Knox to go to that silly restaurant in Times Square to "observe" her. She came in wearing a trench coat and ugly bright-pink trainers like she had dressed in the dark. But I looked past that because she was pretty. Then she did an impression of a panting dog. Funny shite! I thought, alright. This bird has a sense of humor! A breath of fresh air from all the uptight gold-diggers who always came around, for sex, which I took, and that was all they, and anyone else, got from me. No loss. They didn't want the real me, anyway. Then as Knox and I were about to ring for a waitress, she came barreling back in. This time wearing practically nothing. Now *this* I could handle.

She was not just a pretty face. She had a body and used it damn well. Shaking her round tits and arse at the crowd to a funny tune. And, yeah, it stirred my cock. Just like every other man in the place. But then she came over to our table with an attitude bigger than those perky tits she'd been showing off. We chatted her up, but she got all weird and looked like she was going to cry. We tried to cheer her, and she got stroppy. If that wasn't enough, she tipped over for no reason and pushed her big arse in my face! I made a joke and she went into a mood and switched tables.

Women. This was the main reason I didn't bother with relationships. Women got too moody. Too clingy. They expected too much too soon. Or then there's the *in it for the money* variety, which this situation stunk with. "I don't need to pay a chick to be with me."

"You're not paying for her to be really with you, it's more of an ongoing publicity acting gig," Raymond chimed in. Oh, the man was smooth.

"I still don't understand why this would work for me. What was wrong with Holly?" I asked him. She was hot and easy to get along with.

Salvatore scoffed. "The problem with *Hannah* was you had sexual relations with her and she stopped working. Need I remind you of the *Daily Mirror* shots of her in the bathroom with coke? She was shopping a story about you when they went with that photo."

He brought out the tabloid paper to show Raymond and slapped it down on the desk.

I tightened my jaw. "You didn't need to show me that again." The tabloids loved putting my name a picture out with crazy shite." They hadn't moved on even though I hadn't been back in the U.K. in months. I wasn't even with her in the picture. My headshot was next to her snorting coke off the seat of a toilet. When you're willing to stoop that low, you got a habit.

She was on coke, she had to go. I partied more in my early days, but now I found anyone that did them pathetic. As for sex, I had her twice. She was the one who tried to sell a relationship that didn't happen. That didn't make her mine.

"You want to be taken seriously? You want to be considered for real acting jobs?" Raymond said. "Then you need to drop the bimbos and change your image. Hollywood will call."

I blew out a breath. Oh, how I loved New York City and its frankness. But on this he was wrong. Hollywood had already come, but I didn't want the stupid roles they offered to me. "What more do they want? I've done everything you asked in public."

All my private charity work had become public self-promotion because of him. I didn't get into charity to take credit. I did it to help people. Giving came from the soul, not with attachments or thoughts of what you could gain from it. Public works diminished its meaning.

"The organizations are all on board with you using your celebrity to promote them. Raymond, we could add that to Brooke's agreement? You attract more people by going public with your celebrity—"

"My image is what you criticize," I interjected.

"No. Your charity image is the one part of your image that shows substance. It's likeable. You need to do more, show you've taken to being a positive addition to celebrity in the U.S. and not the rock star lifestyle of the U.S."

"I've been vetting you for roles on Broadway," Raymond said. "With more lessons, I may be able to add you as a special edition for a show. Invite some producers. Get the right publicity. It could do wonders should you decide to move on to L.A., and Brooke knows the ins and outs of the city. She can help there too."

"She agreed to do all this?" I asked him.

"Of course she did. She jumped at the chance," he

answered. Raymond had said everything he thought I'd want to hear. I wasn't convinced. "I haven't agreed to do any of this and I'll be leaving if she doesn't get here in the next five minutes."

He was on his phone then. Brooke wasn't scoring any endearing points.

But, as if on cue, she came rushing through the door. Her ginger hair brushed the top of her long neck. She had on a knit shirt, snug across her tits, and fitted jeans on her hips. She was curvy. Sexy. Everything alright. But there were those hideous scuffed-to-hell trainers on her feet again. That bothered me. My family was working class—we didn't have much. But the one thing my father made sure I got was proper shoes on my feet. That was going to have to change.

Her eyes went to mine and her tongue darted out her mouth over her glossy lips. She would look good sucking me off. But that I'd keep to myself for now. Overall, she was well fit. "Sorry I'm late. Cinder, the apartment cat, got out, and I helped my landlord catch her and bring her back in."

I stood and held out my hand. "Ms. Sullivan."

Brooke appeared shocked I knew her name, and her cheeks pinked.

"Mr. Pierce." She folded her arms to cover her tits. Then it was as if the bells went off in her head and she practically stuck them out and lifted her chin. I supposed she remembered she had to sell the act.

I chuckled and shook my head. Brooke Sullivan was a peculiar woman. She wasn't boring, and that was intriguing. She might make this stupid plan interesting.

CHAPTER
FOUR

Brooke

I didn't know if I was upset because Dylan was laughing at me or because I was acting like a teen with a first crush around him. I didn't blush. I wasn't inhibited. I performed half-naked in the musical *Hair* in college. Never mind that my father intervened and forced me to quit. The way Dylan looked at me bothered me.

I mean, men have looked at me before, but not the way he did. My mom called it something cheesy, like "bedroom eyes." His eyes roamed all over my body like he was imagining touching me intimately. It was carnal. Bold. Dirty. And what made it worse was that I wanted to have all that, and that wasn't me. It wasn't what I came here for. This was a job. I was a professional. I'd never be another one of his many, many female conquests.

Raymond's hands pressed down on my shoulder, keeping me in place. "Let's just sit down and relax?"

"I am relaxed. I don't understand what's so funny," I said in annoyance.

"You, a grown woman, blushing every time I look at you." Dylan answered like I had asked him.

I pursed my lips. "A gentleman would have ignored it."

"We both know I'm no gentleman," he said. "And I didn't say I didn't like it."

I snorted. "I didn't ask if you did." I turned to Raymond and shook my head.

Raymond beamed. "No, this is perfect. The blossoming beginnings." He went back behind his desk and leaned back in his seat. "A young wholesome—"

"Down to earth," I said over him.

"Pretty young lady." Raymond winked at me. "It is only right that the new budding relationship has a bit of fascination. You are an unknown dating a celebrity."

"This can't take long. I need to get to practice before the game," Dylan said.

I glanced over at him. He didn't look like he was ready for a game. He looked like he was ready to go out. He had on a button-down shirt, tight, fitted jeans, and a pair of fancy sneakers that looked like you'd need instructions to lace them up. His shirt was opened enough to give a peek at his chest and the top of a colorful tattoo that was showing. They must have air-brushed that out in the photos. The design looked colorfully intricate. I flicked my eyes up to his face and bit the inside of my cheek. The impact was full on now. His pale blue eyes had flecks of gold through them. They were dazzling. His hair was pulled back again and, God, that face. He was stunning.

"You want a closer look, I'll give you one," Dylan purred.

Pig. I turned my head away, schooling my features to show that his remark did not affect me. He was cocky, but I really needed this job. "So what exactly would we do?"

"Be natural. Go out around town. Go on dates. See shows. Do some charity work. You need to be seen. I'll leak where you will be to the press. Click," Raymond said, gesturing like he was taking photos. "The more buzz the higher your profiles. Brooke has a stellar background here. She doesn't even have a parking ticket. So you are in good hands."

"So let's go over the details," Salvatore said.

"I haven't agreed to anything," Dylan replied, his gaze steady on me.

I hunched my shoulders.

"I didn't say no, either. Let's talk about it," he added.

"Yes, let's. Here are the contracts." Salvatore handed over documents to me and him. My mouth dropped open, and I quickly covered it up with a cough at the initial shock of the amount. The money was more than I made at my job in two months, though the assignment was on a trial basis to last for six weeks. After that time, we would have to meet again for re-negotiation. "They are pretty standard. You will cover her trip expenses if you need for her to travel to your away friendlies or England. We will be going to Toronto, Seattle and L.A.—the rest will be here."

"I'll probably go back to Manchester for my dad's birthday. But I'm going alone. I don't want my mum getting ideas—no offense," he said.

"None taken," I replied. "I may visit home in Seattle, alone, too."

Dylan nodded.

My mom would be thrilled. She had always been supportive. But my father? I could only imagine what my father would say to me dating an athlete. *You're trying to marry into money.* Hell, the entire situation would make him think I was taking the easy road. I shook my head at the thought.

"Anything else?" Raymond asked.

"Rocco is still in Britain. He will arrive next week," Dylan said.

Salvatore typed into his phone.

I lifted my brow. "Who's Rocco?"

Dylan glimpsed at me. "Rocco's my dog," he explained.

I perked up in my seat. Doggie! "I'd love to meet Rocco... I mean, taking him out might be a good photo op. It could raise awareness for animal shelters."

"Sorry. My dog is personal," he said.

"Of course." I stared at my hands. "Apologies."

"She will need clothes," Dylan added.

"I've got clothing," I said, straightening my back.

It wasn't a lie. I had left the designer clothes my parents had bought me when I packed up and left for New York.

"Then why are you wearing those trainers—I mean, athletic shoes, sneakers?" Dylan clarified.

"I'm familiar with the British term... I wear them because they're comfortable," I mumbled. I couldn't bring myself to mention the perfectly good ones I left at home out of guilt.

He looked at Salvatore and an unspoken conversation passed between them.

"Okay, well, here is the nondisclosure agreement," Salvatore said, presenting it to me. "You don't need to go over it. It's standard. It's to avoid any negative press."

"The press does follow me around. I'm out living my life," Dylan said with irritation in his voice.

I looked over at Raymond. "Of course you both don't have to worry. I can and will be professional."

"So how about we sign and start?" Raymond asserted.

Dylan shook his head. "I'm not signing until I get to talk to her alone first."

"Why?" Salvatore asked. He lowered his voice, but we could both hear him. "We agreed there will be absolutely no sexual relations. We will need this to last the full six weeks. Then review."

My face warmed. I glanced Dylan's way.

His lips turned up into a lazy smile as his eyes raked over my body. "I never agreed to that."

"Stop teasing her, Dylan." Salvatore scowled.

I shifted in my seat. "You don't have to worry, Salvatore. I promise I won't be having sex with Dylan."

"Good. We'll be right outside the door." They rose.

Raymond gave me his thumbs-up and I returned it, though I was nervous as they closed the door behind them, leaving me alone with Dylan.

"I don't want to do this." He rose and started to pace the length of the room. "I'm sure you don't want to do it either."

I smiled as my bottom lip trembled. "Honestly, I'm not sure, but I'm willing to give it a try."

He stopped near my chair. "I like that. Honesty. I expect it all the time. I don't tolerate liars."

"Neither do I," I agreed. Though I did believe in little ones.

"So you understand this is a job. It won't end with roses and romance or anything. I will do what is needed in public."

"I can act," I said. "I have no interest in romance either. I'm in it for—"

"The money," he finished. His tone was clipped.

I crossed and uncrossed my legs. "No, actually I could use the money to help with the time away in between work. But I'm in it, just like you, for the career possibilities."

"Good," he said and touched his chin. "So if anyone asks how we met?"

I licked my lips. "We'll say... you saw me yesterday and—"

"You stuck your butt in my face," he said and laughed.

"Grow up," I grumbled. "That kind of stuff will set the pace off wrong for what we are trying to do here. How about we say we met at the restaurant or we can set it up that we meet for the first time at a game?"

My hair fell forward across my face. Our hands met and there was that jolt of electricity at his touch. I moved my head back and quickly tucked my hair behind my ear.

"We'll keep it simple." His eyes fluttered over me. "We met at the restaurant and I heard you sing and it was... beautiful."

I tilted my head down and smiled.

"So cute," he softened.

My pulse sped up. I tried not to tremble when he brushed his hand under my chin before dropping his hands back by his sides. He walked over to the window.

I stood. "Great, I'll call them back in."

"Not yet." He stood up and faced me. His gaze was intense. "We should start by me touching you more."

My lips parted and my pulse sped up. "More in what way? No."

"You're not a virgin or a prude. I saw that dance number," he said.

I pursed my mouth. "I'm no virgin prude, but it was a dance, and a dance is an act."

"But you blush like one. If someone is going to be convinced that we're together, you need to act natural around me. Being a girlfriend means touching. We must rehearse," he explained.

"Uhm…" He had a point. I was a professional. "Well, alright."

"Come to me," he commanded, his voice a deep, low rumble that was crazy-sexy.

I felt a tightening low in my body. My legs wobbled a little. My brain tapped in, *what are you, a dog to fetch? Make him come to you.* "No, you come to me."

He smirked. "So you want to play difficult? I don't date difficult women."

"Why, because my cup size is smaller than my head?" I slapped my hands over my mouth.

"There's nothing wrong with big boobs. You one of those women-haters?" he asked.

I jutted my chin. "No. I'm pro women, but I doubt anyone will believe I'm your type."

"Then you need to act like you are," he said simply. "Now, get over here."

Shit. His command was panty-melting. I took a step. "We should talk some more. I need to know you more."

"Now it feels like every relationship I've ever had," he said.

"You've been in a few?" I asked. "What was your longest one?"

"You don't know?" he said sarcastically. "You seem familiar with tabloids."

I bit my lip. "Fair enough. I don't know you and I want to... I mean, I should get to know something about you first. My longest relationship was five months."

"Three for me. My career comes first and it always will," he said.

"Same here," I said. Why was I stalling? I didn't have much time left to stall. Dylan had had enough.

"For fuck's sake, woman." He took wide steps between us. "I touch what I want whenever I want. That's how it is with me and my women," he said bluntly.

"I'm not that kind of woman..." I said, my back hitting the wall. "I may be playing a role, but my character is different than your usual. I'll...adjust to public displays of affection, but I will put on the brakes if I think it's too much or out of character."

He cocked his head to the side and caged me in. His hands were on my shoulders.

"See, you're trying to control how I behave with you and I don't take orders. You need me, too. So you're going to have to learn to go with it."

A ripple of excitement shot through me as he

advanced. And before I could say another word, he gripped my waist and pulled me hard against his body, his lips crashing down against mine, ultra-soft and warm. My lips parted, and he slid his tongue in my mouth with a lingering minty taste. His tongue dueled with mine, igniting heat from every sensual glide of its touch. His kiss sang through my veins all the way down to my toes. I was shocked by the eagerness of my response. My hands moved to grip his neck, wanting more. I'd been kissed, but he showed me that all kisses weren't equal. He had skill. Finesse. It felt too good to stop, so I didn't.

He made this sexy hum in the back of his throat as he pressed in for more, and I was so ready to give it to him. His hand gripped my waist tight, and he pulled me harder against his front. I could feel the bulge of his erection straining against his jeans. This was too much. Too fast and way too soon. This was my job.

I moved back, and he immediately broke away, leaving me sucking in air as I fought to catch my breath. I knew without looking that my face was flushed, not only with desire, but embarrassment that he could arouse me and have me lose myself so easily, too. I was disappointed in myself.

I touched my cheeks. "Thanks for the practice. I can't seem to stop blushing. I'll work on it."

"No, leave it. I like it," he said in a soft tone. He cleared his throat. "It looks more natural." He stepped back. His eyes clouded over and he straightened his clothing. "I need to prepare for the match. You familiar with football?"

"Not overly," I admitted. Dylan went to the door, and

I had a few seconds to straighten up my hair and clothes before Raymond and Salvatore came back inside the office. I had my poker face on, but the air had left the room. And there was no doubt something had happened between us.

Dylan didn't bother. He went over to the desk and signed the contract. "Get her new trainers and bring her to the tunnel after the game," he said to Salvatore, then walked out without a backward glance. I couldn't help myself from turning and watching Dylan as he went through the door.

I sighed. What had I gotten myself into?

"I'll be downstairs." Salvatore shook Raymond's hand and left.

I signed the contract and was about to leave when Raymond called me back.

He frowned. "Remember, this is a job. I don't want you getting hung up on him. He is a player. He can act too, you know. That's why I'm representing him. So keep your head together."

I nodded. "You don't have to worry about me. I will handle it," I said, watching Dylan walk out the door.

How? I wasn't exactly sure, but this was my first break. I wasn't going to blow my chance.

CHAPTER

FIVE

I convinced Salvatore to stop at my place to pick up my guilt-ridden pair of pink Chuck shoes, and we set out for the New York City F.C. soccer match at Yankee Stadium in the Bronx. The team shared the stadium, probably because of the limited real estate space available to accommodate the team in the vastly populated metropolis. According to Salvatore, whom I easily chatted with in the back of a Lincoln Town Car, it was also because American football and baseball were well-established sports staples in the U.S.

Part of Dylan's marketing appeal was his European football club stardom, since his good looks, charisma and determination could get more American sport enthusiasts to demand more televised broadcasting of soccer games. He was already in negotiations with several sports broadcasting networks to have him work as an on-air commentator. The popularity could bring out more demand and, in the long term, eventually a home stadium of their own in New York.

I wasn't sure about Dylan being the spokesperson to improve soccer's popularity. Sure he had the good looks, but he was also overtly confident and cocky. He had a tendency to tease in a way that irritated me. When he wasn't doing that, he was lustfully staring at my body, completely throwing me off my game. He was already taking control and testing the boundaries of our agreement by the way he had kissed me.

The way I reacted to his kiss could have come from my lack of experience with men like him. Growing up, I had crushes on jocks and secretly put hearts with their names on my notebooks, although I pretty much dated in the theater crowd. No jock in my high school would ever be caught in the section of the lunchroom near us, let alone invite one of us to dances. A guy like Dylan Pierce wouldn't look at me. But now I had a role to play his woman.

I'd done acting workshops where I'd pretended to be in a relationship. Never for a minute did I forget what I was doing during the scene. Never had I allowed myself to get carried away. But those moments with Dylan alone, being in his arms for a few minutes... I felt desired, passion. Raymond was right, he was a dangerous player, and I could be playing a dangerous game with my heart. I would rein it in and assert my own control next time. I would, and could, distance myself. I would be able to keep this job.

"So this is your first live soccer game?" Sal asked.

From his expression, I could see he had asked me twice.

"Yes, though my roommate, Gemma, is from London. She's an Arsenal fan."

He made a face, and we laughed. "Keep that one to yourself. Dylan is—was—Manchester City through and through. I mean, if you could have seen him in his prime… He was amazing. Don't get me wrong, Dylan's still a great forward. F.C. is lucky to have him, but careers in sports come and go. They don't last forever."

"And that's why he's on to acting?" I asked in a light tone.

"Yeah. He has been taking lessons here in New York," he replied.

My brows lifted. "Oh, he has? With who?"

He looked puzzled. "I don't know specifically, but I know he's good. He gets scripts sent too. He's holding out for more serious roles with bigger budgets."

"Action films?" I asked.

"Raymond says you have been in a couple of films."

I blew out a breath and smiled. "Yeah. I have, but nothing you've probably seen."

My roles were as extras on a couple of horror movies and a dancing background girl on a peppy pharmaceutical commercial.

"Well, you may have an opportunity here," he said brightly. "Now, I'll be taking you to the private suite, but during the game we will move you down where the team leaves seating. You may see some celebrities, corporate sponsors, wives and girlfriends. You just act natural and try not to get in too deep with conversations since you both haven't spent much time rehearsing. Perhaps, in time, you may be able to influence Dylan away from partying."

"I don't know if I can do that," I replied.

"Well, another voice of conscience could do him good. Some of his friends on the team are still in the full-on party phase. Dylan has a reputation, as you know."

"Yeah," I said.

"Something, with your help, we could change," he said and smiled. "I don't mean in any sexual way. I'd prefer to keep the business part going. With Dylan, sex often complicates things. He usually has sex and dumps them. We hired you in hopes that you would keep your relationship with him professional."

"I will. Thanks," I said.

"Sorry, but he can be persuasive. I mean, we had to change a few publicists recently because he had sex with them and they became upset with him when it went nowhere. I don't want to have to find someone else to replace you, especially after the two of you go public. Believe me, your life is about to change."

I could only imagine. My phone beeped with a text message. I checked, and it was from my mother.

A.M. Starling67: Dad told me you had a job? Is this one of your little lies?
You don't have to be so proud. You're always welcome at home.

"You alright?" Sal asked.

I smiled, though my stomach muscles knotted. I'd need to speak with Raymond later about getting an advance. But that wouldn't happen if I didn't bring it today. I was determined to do whatever was needed to secure this job and get control of my finances once and for all.

We pulled up to the curb and waited for the driver to come around to open the door. Salvatore immediately went to his phone, leaving me to take in the scene. The line of sports fans stretched the length of the sidewalk and around the corner. Some were wearing the official blue and white team jerseys and carrying signs for the game. One read, "Dylan, will you marry me?"

I smiled. Dylan Pierce wasn't the marrying kind. Salvatore and Raymond had pretty much spelled that out for me. Dylan himself said there wouldn't be any hearts and flowers at the end of this gig.

Salvatore motioned me forward, and we followed a security guard through a staff door, up an elevator and down a carpeted corridor, which was decorated with team photos and jerseys, to the stadium's private suite. I'd been in plenty of suites before with my parents at various charity events. This suite had cloth-covered tables and a full bar that were occupied by casually dressed celebrities and corporate suits. There were full-staffed buffet tables with designer-clad wives and trendily dressed children who were filling their plates. Along the wall was a panoramic view of the stadium where staff were preparing the field for the game.

"You'll need to start here," Salvatore said in a quiet tone. "I'll introduce you and pick you up next to the tunnel to the locker rooms after the game."

He handed me my VIP passes and introduced me to two females seated with a teen with Beats headphones over his ears at a table nearby. Chloe was the overdressed brunette with a full face of makeup. Kayla was an African

American with wavy hair and a team jersey. James was her son, who gave me a little wave before returning to his music.

The brunette's eyes flicked over me from head to toe before I sat down in my seat. Her smile lasted the length it took for Salvatore to move away from the table. "You're a friend of Dylan Pierce? Where is Hannah, his girlfriend?"

Mental note: ask Dylan about Hannah later. Deal with bitchiness now.

"I don't know who Hannah is and, frankly, I don't care," I said, leaning forward in my chair. "And yes, I'm here for Dylan."

"You part of a Make-A-Wish program or something?" she pressed.

"Chloe, come on," Kayla said.

I flicked my eyes over her and wrinkled my nose. "I was about to ask the same thing about you, but I wouldn't want to insult the people in need. In fact, I'm flattered to be thought of as part of such an amazing group of people who've been honored by the program."

Chloe blinked at me. "I wasn't making fun of…never mind."

Kayla smiled at me. "Oh, she's definitely with Dylan. He always has a smart remark to say back. Salvatore introduced her. He would know."

I turned away dismissively and leaned toward Kayla. "Dylan and I haven't talked much about the team. Would you fill me in, please?"

Chloe rose. "I'll see you later, Kayla."

I shrugged. *Good.*

"Brooke, did he say?" I nodded. "Nice to meet you.

I'm Lance's wife. Lance is a mid-fielder like Knox, Erik, and Rico. Chloe is with Tyler. She used to be with Erik from the team."

"Too bad for Tyler and Erik," I said.

She laughed. "I like you. You'll have to be able to handle yourself in this world. Some of us actually enjoy the game, while others come just to be seen. Which one are you?"

She was nice, and I hated lying, but that was what I had to do. So I answered, "I'm here for the game and Dylan." I kept a small smile on my lips. There was truth in what I said. After meeting Dylan and, well, kissing him, I got a taste of his passion and wanted to see how his intense energy translated on the field. It would be good for my job, of course, to understand him better.

She beamed. "Oh, good. Then you can come and sit by us. We go to as many matches as we can."

A waitress came over and filled the glass before me with Chardonnay. I picked up a club sandwich and ate, while Kayla spoke and filled me in on all the players' positions and plays. It was like having live *CliffsNotes*. Besides, I enjoyed the way in which she talked about Lance. She was in love. He seemed like a good guy, and I couldn't wait to meet him. I sighed. There I was again, getting ahead of myself and attached to people I didn't even know yet.

"You meet anyone from the team?" she asked.

"Just Knox," I said.

The corner of her mouth curved upward. "I'd say stay as far away from Knox as you can, but you're with Dylan so you must like to party too."

I giggled. "A little."

"Well they party a lot," she said. "Would be good for Dylan to slow down like Lance has with us."

An announcement came on, and after Kayla got her son's attention we were escorted by a guard down to our seats. I had never sat so close to the front. Truthfully, I never had that much interest in sports. The area where we sat wasn't as occupied as the other sections of seating. Still, the stadium was practically full, with the monitor displaying an image of the team and their opponent, D.C. United.

After a flourishing high soprano sang the national anthem, the teams took the pitch. Secretly, I wished their shorts were shorter. They were all mighty fine and I would have said so, but I didn't know Kayla well enough yet to know how she'd take it. The crowd cheered as each one was announced, but when Dylan came on, the crowd went into a frenzy. I jumped up too and clapped, to the humor of Kayla. She said, "He's like Lance, all about the game. Save your energy."

Dylan did a quick wave and jogged over to the inner circle where the referee was stationed. Kayla went straight into a chant that I caught onto quickly and joined.

"Score! They win. We're freaking dynamite! NYC!"

New York F.C. won the toss and Dylan kicked off the match. Seeing a live game and watching one on TV were two different things. The ninety minutes went by in a flash. Dylan and the team dominated the ball and had D.C. on defense throughout the game. Truly, Dylan stole the show. He was a machine. Driven. Passionate. No one on the other team was able to get the ball from him once he had it, or could successfully stop him from taking it back from them once he wanted it.

When it was all said and done, he had managed to be a big part of the three winning goals that won their 3-to-1 match. The crowd erupted and I was right with them. And this wasn't his prime? I was thoroughly impressed.

I was on my feet before I could even think about it and rushing down with Kayla to the F.C. sideline, where I saw Dylan moving with his teammates off the field. He skimmed the crowd and when he zeroed in on me, he set a beeline toward where I stood waiting for him. Everything else seemed to shrink as he moved in my direction. This was the beginning of our act. This was our scene.

His hair was slicked back with sweat. His shirt clung to his body, outlining the sculpted plains of his chest. His gorgeous face was set in fierce concentration as he walked over to me.

My heart pounded hard against my rib cage. I pepped myself up—I could do this.

As soon as he reached me, he didn't hesitate to take me. His strong hands locked around my waist and pulled me hard against his body, causing a shiver to race up my spine.

I threw my arms around his neck and entwined my leg with his as he covered my lips with a hard kiss. The touch of his lips set off sparks of sensations throughout my body, his tongue tangling with mine in deep, massaging caresses. It was electric, and I was caught up in the current. My body molded against his and those strong, manly hands moved down to my ass, and squeezed. The hum of the crowd rose higher, bringing me back to earth and our agenda. I became aware, and a bit self-conscious, of all the flashes from the surrounding cameras. This was all really happening!

We broke the kiss and Dylan cupped my face. Bending his head close to my ear, he said, "Alright, Ms. Sullivan?"

A moan escaped my lips. I'd say that and then some, but I had to reel it in. "You know it."

"Damn, I'd fuck you right here if I could." That had me swiping him playfully. He had gone too far. He grabbed my hand and moved it back around my waist for another kiss. Was he overacting? It felt good, so I went with it. Because, damn, was he good at it. We parted, and he smoothed my hair back in place. I felt a light brush of his lips against my forehead and then he held me at arm's length.

"There it is," he cooed while kissing my cheek.

I didn't have to think about it. My blush was there, and it worked. The press and the crowd gathered around were loving it. Placing his arm around me, he pretended to shield me from the photographers. In truth, they probably had a bazillion photos by now.

I hid my face in the crook of his neck as he led me off toward the tunnel to the locker rooms. Just as we were about to turn in, a woman in short-shorts, a tank top, and wearing bright red lipstick pressed forward. She grabbed Dylan and was just about to plant a kiss on his face when I stepped in between them, making her smear a glossy mess across my nose. She moved back and Dylan whispered, "What are you doing?"

When we moved a couple steps away, I said, "Uhm...I decided my character is territorial."

He chuckled and pulled off his shirt and my mouth salivated. Biceps, triceps, that sexy V at the hips... *Hot damn.* His tattoo was of a crest and dragon. It was beautiful. He lifted the end of the shirt and wiped at my nose.

"EEK. Sweat," I protested, suddenly grossed out. Well, the kissing had stopped.

Dylan pointed out as much. "I'm all over you. This is the least of your worries."

I was struck dumb, dazzled for a few seconds. "What?"

He grinned. "Stop fucking me with your eyes. Or I'll take you up on it."

I fixed my face, and he chuckled.

"Under other circumstances I might be offended," he said in a way that made it clear he wouldn't be. "But I know I fuck as well as I play. Never disappoint."

"So do I," I bragged. He eyed me curiously, and gave me a hooded look.

I lifted my chin and left him to wonder.

"Anyway, you want to look like a clown on your photos tomorrow? You've got a red nose."

That made me quiet and I let him finish cleaning it off. I could just imagine the *Daily News* headline: *"Dylan Pierce Bonkers for Bozo the Clown Yank,"* and I told him as much.

He laughed. A deep, tantalizing rumble. He moved back from me. "I mustn't disappoint my fans, though."

He went over to the woman and signed her top, though not on her tits like she wanted. There were other members of his team doing the same thing, and Dylan did sign some other fans' programs and balls. However, the red lipstick female still hung around. And he chatted with her, and the way she was smiling and laughing had me wondering if he was making an arrangement to meet her later.

My stomach flipped over, but I stood my ground, only turning away for a moment to powder my face, should another photo op come. He then moved to do an on-air camera interview and I moved back some more, bumped right into someone heading past me.

"Hello." I turned and found one of his team members standing in front of me. He had a crew cut and big brown eyes. He was smiling. "I'm Tyler."

I smiled and shook his hand. "Brooke. Nice to meet you."

"If it was me, I wouldn't leave you here waiting," he flirted.

I giggled. "It's alright."

"No, it isn't. A beautiful woman like you should never be left waiting," he said smoothly.

I opened my mouth to speak but felt a hand at my elbow. It was Dylan, back at my side. His hand was possessively placed in the small of my back. "Move on."

Tyler laughed as he walked away. "Hope to see you again, Brooke."

"What's that about?" I asked.

"Don't play coy with me. You're mine—pretending to be, at least—and I never share," he said.

I shrugged. "It was a polite conversation. Relax. I know why I'm here, just like you."

Dylan's eyes flashed and his square jaw clenched. "Good. Then don't go off script."

I pressed my lips together. Script. Yes. I needed a reminder, this was fake. "You too."

We stared hard at each other. His friend Knox approached and stepped between us. "Country girl with the sparkly sneakers. You coming to my party tonight?"

Dylan answered "yes" and I answered "no" at the same time.

He pulled me aside. "What's wrong?"

"We shouldn't… Salvatore—"

"Salvatore doesn't control me or us," he hissed, and took a deep breath. "Besides, me becoming less social would be suspicious."

"What type of party? Is it at a nightclub or house?" I asked. I'd have to dress accordingly.

"House. But I expect a dress and heels. Something tight to show off those tits. Wait," he said, glancing over at Knox, who was looking on in amusement. "On second thought, keep the neckline modest."

"I didn't ask for advice on what to wear. I asked location. I'll wear whatever I want to wear," I said with snark.

He moved in really close, brushing his body against my front. "Behave."

My traitorous nipples started to harden. Not good when I was pissed. Dylan, of course, looked down. A smug grin formed across his full lips. No doubt patting himself on the back. He'd won this round.

Salvatore finally appeared, and I moved on over to him.

"I'm sending a car for you tonight," Dylan said with bass in his tone. He came over and kissed my cheek before disappearing into the locker room.

My stomach fluttered and I ran my hand over it soothingly.

Oh, he was a good actor, indeed.

CHAPTER
SIX

Dylan

I stood under the shower's spray and tried to cool off both heads. Brooke was testing me. I hadn't even spent that much time with her, but I hadn't been able to get her off my mind after we kissed in the office. Well, let's be real. I kissed her. I gave her one of my kisses. The one that makes a woman beg for more. I, at first, just wanted to loosen her up, but then she started squirming and rubbing her tits against my chest. Pressing her soft body against my cock. I had to fight with my dick not to take more. I wanted more of her. Even when she stopped me, I knew she was hot and wet. She wanted me. But we were being professional. I understood, and once again pulled back.

At the end of the game, I went to give her a kiss like we had sort of rehearsed. But I don't know. She was all cute and sweet. The way she jumped all over me. It was like she was genuinely happy about the game, and me. I'd seen plenty of players who had that. Someone waiting on the sides to see them. Never me. I didn't want to lead anyone on. But she did seem excited to be there.

Happy for me, even. Then, she went rogue and was all over me. Kissing and rubbing up against me. Once again, teasing my dick for all to see. I, a professional, went with it. When I calmed down and went to do fans and press, I turned my back for a minute, only to find her over and chatting up that arsehole, Tyler. What was she thinking? What if the press decided that was a better story? Then we'd both be arsed out. Fucking Tyler knew not to mess with mine. Mine? I shook my head. What the hell was I thinking? She went from all sweet and innocent to a fiery little cock tease. What does she need my help for, anyway? I'd hand her over a BAFTA. Well done.

I shook my head and washed my body. She was pretending to be mine, and she needed to behave as such. But I showed her. Two can tease. Her nipples were poking into me just from me brushing against her. Her breath had come faster just from me standing close to her. I could tease too. She'd learn to behave with me.

What the fuck am I doing?

I wiped the water from my face and frowned. Not only did I not understand her, but I was spending time trying to figure her out. I didn't do that with women. They did that with me, and I didn't give them much but a good fuck. But Brooke made me want to talk to her, and she did these cute things like blushing and hiding her face against my neck. She was bringing out some protective shite I never try with women. If they go, and few have, they didn't get to come back. End of. It didn't take long for them to realize they'd lost the best. I didn't play second. I was always first.

My coaches always said that women would come later. Fit women. Hot, sexy ones. And yeah, they did come. And I had a lot of them. The more I rose in my career, the more women came a-running. Practically falling all over themselves to get to me. Not just because of my big cock. It was because of what I did with my big cock. I knew how to please them. I knew how to make them beg me for more. And it was fun at first—getting everyone I wanted—but then when I reached the top of my game, I got the dramatic women who tried to blackmail me or trick me into marrying them. Now, I just enjoyed sex. I loved sex, but I never wanted them around. But now I had agreed to pretend to bring Brooke in. She proved herself good at the job today, too. There was going to be a learning curve. Despite it all, I wanted her to continue. But she had to learn not to play with me.

"Hey, man, what're you doing? You spacing out?" Knox called to me.

"Ha. Nice one," I said sardonically.

Bullocks. The water had run cold. I rinsed off and grabbed my towel. Brooke had me all messed up. I wished that I hadn't invited her to the party tonight. I needed to regroup. Set myself back in control.

I got dressed. My body was tired, and I needed a rest. I could get a massage. Someone to come over and give me a happy ending too. I had a massage therapist, but I fucked that up. Hell, I was running out of women, to tell the truth. And now I had to be good. But if Salvatore thought I wasn't fucking, he had lost his mind. I'd never pay for pussy, so escorts were out. But I was getting someone. And soon.

"So you think Brooke will be cool tonight?" Knox asked.

"Why wouldn't she be?" I replied.

"Well, I'm bringing the crew." That was code for a bunch of ballers. Women who would do whatever and kept their mouths shut for the most part.

"Cameras?" I reminded him.

"Damn, cameras are getting tinier. We could make them strip at the door?" Knox mused, but knowing him he would do it.

I sighed. "You do that and I can't bring Brooke."

"That country girl got you whipped already? You tapped that pussy yet?" he teased.

He was taking a piss. I didn't bother answering.

"She is awful cute in that sweet girl-next-door kinda way. I'd like to taste that."

"Don't talk *tosh*. You won't touch her," I gritted out.

"Why not?" he asked.

I tightened my jaw. "Do not test me."

Knox was sort of my mate. He was alright, most of the time we hung out. We partied, but that was all we did together. Party and play football and get pussy. He was alright, though. He was a couple years younger than me. He had about that much time left in football. I was more like him up until I crossed the pond and came to end my career at New York F.C. In truth, I couldn't afford to be. I wasn't going to sit around and do nothing when I retired. I was going to get another career.

Knox held up his hands. "Easy, man, you are crazy-uptight. I was joking. Lance will show with his wife. Tyler and Erik. Maybe Jordan and Ash will be there too," he said. "I was just setting up for later when you send her home. I'll keep a couple girls you want to have back for you. Or send them over to your place."

"I'll think about it," I said, and he left it, knowing I wasn't serious. I didn't need him to get me women. I didn't need to deal with him and try to fix my career. But in a way he was right. The best way to get past this shite with Brooke was to fuck someone else. Keep her where I needed her to be—for work.

I left and drove back to my place on 70th. I didn't really know if this was where I wanted to be, but the location was good. And near Central Park, where I ran in the mornings. I looked over at the dog bed by the row of windows in my new, modern flat. I had everything almost set for Rocco. My parents got him properly chipped and vaccinated. He should arrive next week. I hated leaving him behind. He was the one thing consistent in my life. My buddy. He'd always been there, even when my family wasn't able to be. My parents were cool, but in truth, my coaches were the ones who had raised me. I loved them and all. And I'd do what I could to make their, and my family's, lives good. But I was always away, training. Rocco was the one thing I had bought for myself a few years ago. He was unconditional in his love and acceptance. He never put any demands on me. The thought crossed my mind to introduce Rocco to Brooke. She had become all excited about meeting him. Something weird went through me as I played out how excited she would be to see him.

No. She was a temporary part of my life. I didn't need him getting attached.

I shook my head, plopped down on my leather couch and turned on the TV. We were playing each other. Maybe Knox was right. I just might take him up on his offer tonight.

CHAPTER
SEVEN

Brooke

By the time I got back to my apartment from Yankee Stadium, it was evening and Gemma was already off to *Les Misérables,* leaving me without anyone to share my big news with. Could I tell her the details about my "relationship" with Dylan? She was my best friend, and I was sure she wouldn't tell anyone. However, the definitive answer came from Raymond in his follow-up call later that evening.

"Absolutely not. This all works on consistency. You must tell everyone you are dating him. No one—including family—must know or suspect a thing. You know celebrity stories are bank. A casual slip could leave us both battling denial that might not be easy to shake. It could affect both of your futures."

I paused between pulling out clothes from my closet. "Of course, you're right. Glad I checked with you."

"Me too, but I called about another issue. Did you search your names on social media when you returned from the stadium today?"

"Not yet." I told him about the party as I turned on my computer.

"I did. The pictures aren't coming across as wholesome. They are calling you the 'mysterious flavor of the month.'"

My mouth went dry. "I don't understand. We kissed and stood next to each other."

"Check," he instructed.

Sure enough, I did a search for Dylan Pierce and there we were along with the by-line "flavor of the month." The press had captured the moment of our kiss. My legs were wrapped around his waist as my hands gripped his neck. His lips were locked to mine, his hands cupping my ass. Just viewing the image sent a delicious shudder of desire through my body. It looked and felt like anything but a sweetheart romance. My face flushed as I tried to gain control of my breathing before offering up a bit of defense. "We'll, uhm…maybe we don't want to be type-casted."

Raymond scoffed. "What made it worse was that you both behaved this way on family day."

I could have pointed out that Raymond hadn't prepped me, but part of acting was finding cues in the situation to set the scene. Still, I offered up the only excuse I had left. "It was our first time together, so we were feeding off each other. You know…in the moment."

"It looks bad, don't do it," he said, speaking over me. He blew out a breath against the phone. "You both need to show some restraint. We want to sell you as a sweet couple. Did you see Tanya Barrington making out with William Croix? No, you saw him doing the romance things. You read books, follow the script. When you jump to hug him, don't put your leg around his waist like you're humping him."

I bit my lip. "You're right. I got this."

"I know and I want this for you, Brooke. You're my favorite client. I want to see you move up. You got the acting chops and the rest of the world deserves to see it."

"I'll do better," I promised as I browsed through more photos. They all looked like we were together, but I did see the "flavor of the month" label on several sites. This wasn't going to be easy. I'd need to last longer than a month if this was going to work. It would work if he weren't so attractive and his touch didn't make my brain take a vacation.

Raymond also shared my analysis.

"The press has been burned by Dylan dumping all his other ladies after a few weeks or a month. You will need to bring something different. I'm thinking you go jogging, walk in the village and get coffee after one of your freelance jobs. Something. Just keep it PG-13. The public will be hungrier to see the two of you together if they have to wonder if you're having sex."

My email alert went off, and I noticed the attached pictures of my new photo composite card had come in and I sent it to Raymond.

"Hmm. These shots show your acting range off well, but I think Q Studios can do better," he replied.

I deflated. That was $2,100 down the drain. "I can't afford them," I answered quietly.

Q Studios was in the top five photographers in New York and their prices started at double the amount. How was I going to keep going?

"You will with this job. I'll put in a deposit for you and I received an advance that I'll transfer to you for incidentals," he added since that was going to be the next thing I asked. "I think I may be able to get you to do some stagehand work for the musical *Rent* next week. I'll call my contact. That might be a good photo-op too. Besides whatever Dylan wants you on besides the games."

I closed my eyes. I had little doubt what Dylan wanted me on. Hell, the pictures told it all. His big cock. I took a deep breath. I needed to focus.

"I'll speak with him tonight…but what if this doesn't work? Can't you just use those cards for now?" I slumped down on the bed.

"Brooke, you know your cards are your resume. They give all the people that matter in this business a snapshot of who you are and what you can do. A bad one will get passed over, but a good one will be shared, discussed, sent up the line to those who can hire you. Self-promotion never stops. It gets even more complicated and expensive as your star rises. This is part of the game of show business. It takes sacrifices and risk. You don't stop when you're on the right track."

"You got an Inspiration App?" I giggled despite it all.

He laughed with me. "You're happy again and that's how I want to leave it for now, however, if you need some support, you just call me."

My insides warmed. Raymond was simply the best and a godsend. "Thank you."

Since I rarely had a reason to dress up between my schedule of running to dance classes and auditions, I took my time curling my hair and slid into in a short-sleeved scoop-neck jersey top with a printed designer tulle skirt that fell just above my knees. I finished off the outfit with a pair of stilettos. I had just enough time to add a little eye makeup and gloss before the text came in to tell me the car service was here.

The streets were bare. My location hadn't been disclosed, making it clear that, just as Raymond had said, the press hadn't bitten yet. We would need to try harder. And I'd need to try to behave around Dylan. No matter how incredible of a kisser he was or how amazing it felt to be in his arms or how much heat filled my body at the thought of being around him again. It was just chemistry since we hadn't had sex. That's all.

Sinking into the leather seats of the luxury car, I smiled. At times I missed the wealthy indulgences I had had with my parents. But when I came to New York, I swore I'd make it on my own. I'd never use their name to get ahead. I needed to know I could manage on my own, without their help. My father often said that the best advice his father ever gave him was to earn it himself. Now that the photos were out, I needed to tell him and my mom. So while we were stuck in traffic on the Brooklyn Bridge, I called home to let them know about my "new beau," Dylan.

"Brooke. Richard, it's Brooke," my mother announced when she answered. Her voice was strained. I could hear movement. She was without a doubt moving out of earshot of my father. "Dad told me about what happened yesterday. He's sorry. Do you need help?"

"No, I don't," I grumbled. "I actually called because I'm dating someone new. His name is Dylan Pierce. He's from England. He's a famous soccer player."

"Oh. Richard, Brooke's dating a guy named Dylan," she yelled out cheerfully. "When did this all happen? I talked to you a few days ago, and you didn't mention anything."

"Yeah. Well, it was something that just happened. I'm actually on my way to see him," I replied.

"Ask her what's she doing for work?" My dad's voice boomed next to her.

"I'm working," I said irritably.

"She's working," my mother replied with just as much frustration. "She hasn't had a date in a very long time and she's all alone out there. We should be happy for her. What's his name again?"

I cleared my throat. "Dylan Pierce. I've got to go."

"Alright, dear. I love you. We both love you. You always have a home with us," she said. Her goodbye had become standard, but sometimes it choked me up. Despite all the sorrow and defeat I would feel if I gave up, Mom still reminded me I had a place with her.

I brushed a tear from the corner of my eye. "I love you both. Talk to you later."

Knox lived in a brownstone in North Park Slope, Brooklyn. I had occasionally visited theaters and a few parties in the neighborhood. Most of the houses I had been inside of were divided into apartments. After I was checked out by a security bouncer, I discovered that Knox had the whole house. It was modernly renovated with recessed lighting, but still had some of its original architectural touches, such as red brick walls, half-moon archways and large fireplaces.

The space was semi-crowded. I cursed myself for not arranging things better with Dylan, but set out to search for him. The first person I ran into was Kayla, who was with a large, muscular male who had to be her husband, Lance. They were talking to Tyler and Chloe, who frowned and tugged Tyler away once she saw me approach them with a wave.

"Glad you made it," Kayla said. "This is Lance," she confirmed as I shook his hand and congratulated him on the New York F.C.'s win.

I smiled. "Me too. Have you seen Dylan?"

"Oh, yeah. He's upstairs with Knox," Lance said.

"I'll help you find him," she offered.

We moved to a carpeted staircase and up to the top floor where a DJ was set up and a small group of people were dancing. It wasn't until we reached the leather couches along the back wall that I found Dylan. He was seated surrounded by women on either side of him. Knox, his trusty sidekick, was there too. He had his own harem of women captivated by whatever he was saying. His attention was occupied by their toned bodies in their designer short dresses.

While Knox had some of the women, the majority of gazes in the room were glued to Dylan, with an undisguised longing for his attention. I'd go so far as to say most appeared besotted. Not just by his gorgeous face—which was perfectly framed tonight by his long blond hair—but because he radiated a powerful masculine vitality that drew everyone around him in like a magnet. He had a fierce, virile potency that was purely sexual. I couldn't look away myself. It was intimidating how he captivated me.

His dark blue shirt complemented his pale blue eyes and dark slacks. His sensual lips were turned up in a smile like he was enjoying whatever the women were saying to him while molded to his side.

Kayla whispered, "Sorry."

I took a deep breath and soothed my souring stomach. I wasn't a dramatic runner who would shrink because he was sitting next to a sexy woman. He was hot and rich. Beautiful women come to guys like him gift wrapped. I wasn't going to go over and cause a scene, either. If a man didn't want me, he could step to the left out of the way for the next one who would. However, this was Dylan. And though this setup looked stupid, he knew I was coming. Was this some kind of message? I knew we weren't together as a real couple. However, this was the situation we'd agreed to, and he could hook-up on his own time.

His eyes found mine and his gaze turned dark and commanding. It said, "come to me." He was mesmerizing.

My knees shook a little, but I remained steadfast in my stance. I forced myself to drag my attention away from him and started lightly chattering with Kayla, sending over my own silent message, "Nope. You come to *me*."

Calvin Harris and Rhianna's *This Is What You Came*

For came on and I started to sway. I loved to dance.

It was Knox who stood and approached us. He leaned over and spoke in my ear.

"He's being a good boy," he said as if I'd asked him to explain Dylan's behavior. "Go on over and kiss and make up so he can be less moody."

"We're not fighting," I said in a light tone. "But if he wants to speak with me, he can come over."

Knox grinned, showing off a set of dimples. "Oh, sweetheart, you really don't have a clue who you're dealing with."

"Brooke?" I turned around to find Tyler. He had on a fitted shirt and jeans. His wavy brown hair was gelled back from his angular face, showing off a row of perfect teeth.

He chuckled. "Nice to meet you again." He reached out his hand to shake mine formally and held on to it until I tugged it gently away.

"Likewise." I glanced at Kayla, whose brows knitted as she stared at him. She leaned over and whispered in my ear. "Be careful. He's supposed to be with Chloe."

I nodded. Tyler's hand brushed my arm in an attempt to pull my attention back to him. "Come on and dance, woman," he said, his tone light. His eyes slid down the length of my body and lingered at my hips before he bit the bottom of his lip in a more than obvious show of checking me out. "You were already dancing by yourself. So come on."

I stopped swaying and folded my arms in a futile attempt to cover whatever body part his roaming eyes lingered on. Even if he weren't with Chloe, his checking me out made me want to take a shower. Still, he was waiting for an answer and I opened my mouth to respond when Knox stepped between us and answered for me.

"She's not dancing with you, dude. You'd better leave her alone," he said to him.

I pressed my lips together. I didn't need a babysitter. "I can answer for myself, thank you."

Tyler's grin broadened. "I only asked this beautiful woman to dance."

"And I told you to move on," Knox said, his voice deepening. "She's Dylan's. You know the rules. We don't touch women that are claimed by our teammates."

I frowned at Knox and couldn't help but poke my finger into his chest. "First of all, I'm not *owned* by anyone." I took that moment to glance over at Dylan, to find him looking at me. But he was still surrounded by his harem of women, and I gritted my teeth when I saw the blonde literally trying to crawl into his lap!

I turned my head to Knox and glared at him. "Two, he sure as hell doesn't look like he is too concerned about me right now."

Stepping around him, I said to Tyler, "Yes. I'll dance with you."

Tyler didn't hesitate to take my arm and move us forward to the middle of the room where the crowd of dancers were. I called back over my shoulder to Kayla, "One dance. I'll be right back."

"Don't worry, I'm going to find Lance," she called back.

We stopped in the middle of the dancing crowd, with Tyler positioning himself behind me. He immediately placed his hands on my hips and pressed himself flush against my back. "Come on, beautiful. Dance with me," he said and laughed. This close, I got a dose of the liquor on his breath. Drunk or not, he was annoying me enough to twist out of his grasp and add space between us.

"Are we dancing or not?" I griped.

"Yeah," he yelled, but he had his hands back on my hips again as we swayed. When I tugged against his hold, he was slower in letting me go this time.

"Get your fucking hands off of her, Tyler, before I break them."

I didn't have to look up to know it was Dylan. I don't know if it was the animalistic growl or the crystal clear threat of steel in Dylan's voice, but whichever it was, Tyler's hands dropped from my hips. Within seconds his hands were replaced by Dylan's, only one of his strong hands slipped around my waist and stopped low on my stomach. This close to him, I could feel the muscles rippling under his shirt, and it sped up my pulse. I inhaled through my nostrils and took in his scent. His smell was intoxicating.

"So he can touch you?" Tyler jeered, bringing my attention back to him.

"That's right," Knox said, coming up to stand next to Dylan but somehow positioning his body in a way that if things got physical, Tyler would have to go through him first.

"Do we have a problem, Ty?" Knox grinned, but it never reached his eyes, which were piercing in their intensity. Up until that point, I'd always thought Knox was the goofy one who wouldn't hurt a fly. I couldn't help but shudder. Perhaps I was wrong.

I rolled my eyes at him, since for all public purposes I was supposed to be with Dylan, but Tyler had a point. Dylan was taking way more liberties with my body than Tyler had done. The bottom of his hand rested just a breath away from the top of my underwear and I wasn't trying to get away. Tyler had tried to do the same thing, and it made my skin crawl. I didn't know what to make of it, but Dylan wasn't conflicted. He tightened his hold on me. He wasn't backing down. "She's with me, so fuck off."

I took a deep breath. I wasn't going back to Tyler, and I honestly didn't want Dylan to move away from me. "He's right. I'm with him."

Tyler's eyes shifted between the two of us and he frowned before turning away. He made a beeline for Chloe, who was sulking at the sidelines.

"Arsehole," Dylan called out at his retreating back. "Stay away from him," he said to me.

I twisted out of his hold. "Why should I? Because he asked me to dance? You were obviously preoccupied with your harem of women. Especially the one who looked like she was about to give you a lap dance."

"They were sitting there next to me while I waited for you. And I guess you missed the part when I removed her from my lap, since you were too busy flirting with that bloody wanker," he said with a growl, putting his hands back around my waist and pressing his lips to my ear. "All you had to do was come over to me. You're still trying to resist coming to me."

I laughed a little. "So you invited me to watch you with other women pawing you and I'm supposed to

AMÉLIE S. DUNCAN

come over to you? I'll tell you now, that's never going to happen."

"What happened over there wasn't planned. Some women are forward and I apologize for that," he said softly and pressed a kiss behind my ear that had my pulse quickening. "By the end of this you will not only come to me, you will be begging to please me." He pressed his lips on my neck.

"Dylan," I said breathlessly, heat surging between my thighs. I wanted to point out it wasn't real, but maybe he thought our roles worked better if we pretended.

"Let's have a look at you," Dylan said as he turned me around to face him. He held me at arm's length, his eyes raking over my body.

"Your top's a little too tight, but your tits look good. Skirt's modest, for me," he said smugly.

He was arrogant. I was about to respond otherwise, but then his hand moved down to rub my ass through my skirt.

"No thong. Lace," he mused.

My sex clenched, and I sucked in my breath. I was losing every bit of professionalism, if I ever had any, with him. He needed to stop flirting and help me. I smiled and casually moved his hand away from my butt. "Stop undressing me with your eyes."

He cocked one of his naturally arched brows. "Undressing? Look again, Brooke. I'm fucking you with them."

He watched me shift from foot to foot, trying hard not to squirm in front of him, and grinned. "I didn't even get started on your legs and heels."

I lowered my brows. "Stop teasing me. So what do you want to do now?"

He placed his hand back firmly on my ass and squeezed. "We can dance."

I glanced around and noticed people watching us, which left me without a choice but to leave his hand where he placed it on me. "Ray said we should tone it down."

"Raymond and Salvatore will not boss either one of us around," he said in a low tone. "We behave naturally. Tonight is a party. There are no cameras. Knox had everyone thoroughly checked."

"How did he check?" I asked. "I didn't get checked."

His eyes danced as he gave me one of his heart-stopping smiles that made mine quicken. "You are playing mine. You don't get touched by anyone but me."

I smirked. "Lucky me."

"Damn right, you are," he bragged.

He led us to the middle of the floor. I loved to dance and was surprised to find Dylan matched my moves. He, like Tyler, was all hands, and I should, but didn't, move to stop him.

When I raised my hands over my head, he was pressed in behind me, his hands sliding down the sides of my breasts and over my hips. When I lowered my hands, he pulled my hips hard against his body and ground his cock—which was no doubt big and thick—against my buttocks. He made me afraid and thrilled at the same time at what he might do if I bent at the waist.

Sexual sparks fired off between us as we moved together in our dance. Every brush of his hand had my body responding, seeking more brushes and more touches.

After a while, my body rose to his touches, welcoming every brush, but found his hands less ready to give them. Damn him. He had me wanting him. So easily.

My breasts were heavy and aching, my clit throbbing and pulsing, my panties completely ruined. I was overwhelmed with lust and was relieved when the music finally changed to a fast tempo that didn't match his erotic torment.

I was so hot and wet that I needed to get away to regain my composure.

"I'll be right back," I said, ready to head for the bathroom, when Dylan's hand gripped my waist and he shook his head.

"You won't be rubbing your pussy and orgasming from what I did to you. That's mine. You want to come; you ask for me to take care of you."

I was wet and aching and all but ready to beg for the very thing I craved. My conscience had left along with the part of my brain that knew this was a job that I could lose by a word from this man. Still, the thought of his long fingers rubbing my clit didn't seem like a completely bad thing. There were no cameras, and we were supposed to be together, anyway. Right? My body wouldn't let me say "no." I wanted him to touch me.

I mumbled, "I don't…know."

Dylan quickly moved me out of the room and off to a quiet, dark corner. People were around, but he stood so close he blocked me from view. So close that his strong thighs pressed against mine. His masculine heat and scent surrounded me.

He inhaled sharply and grunted. "You look good and

smell good, Brooke. I bet you taste good too. You want me to stroke your pussy? If I stroke it, I will taste it, if I taste it, I'll devour it. I'll slide my tongue all over your pussy before I fuck you with it. Tell me you want it."

I moaned as a shudder worked through my body. I could feel the arousal on my thighs, which were slightly agape. I was drowning in his crass words, the call of his body. I wanted him badly, but this situation wasn't casual. This was work. I tried to remind him, to get him to help us. "Dylan…we shouldn't."

His hand slid between our bodies, smoothing down the front of my skirt. He hissed as he pressed his fingers in and right up against my clit. "Say you want it and I'll do it right here," he said in a low tone.

"No. Please. Not here," I said breathlessly. I tried to muster some anger to stop my need to come. "I don't want to come in a hallway. We need to stop."

"I won't take you here," he said as his finger teased against my clit through the fabric, and I moaned, fighting hard not to open my legs and give him full access.

"We can't," I said.

"Why not? We are dating and we can't be seen with anyone else. No one will know but us."

I gripped his hand. *So he wants to touch me out of convenience? What a charmer.* My twisting and moving around him caught him off guard and I took that opportunity to rush away.

He had my arms before I could get far. "Don't run. Talk to me," he commanded. He turned me around to face him.

I dropped my head to try to school my face but

couldn't. I didn't do vulnerable.

Dylan captured my chin and lifted it, scrutinizing my expression. "What did I say that has you looking upset now?"

"Nothing. Salvatore and Ray don't expect you to be a saint with me, just discreet. I've got an idea for your character. You have sex behind my back to preserve the purity we share." My lip slightly trembling was the only thing that gave me away as I plastered on a smile.

He gave me a confused look. "What are you talking about?"

He wasn't going to drop it so I told him the truth.

"It was nothing. I don't do sex for convenience's sake. I want to be touched because a man wants to touch me. Not because he doesn't want to do without," I said, and flicked my gaze away.

He sighed and gripped my arms. "Look at me."

I stared up at him and sighed.

"I was trying to get you to agree because I want to touch you and I know you want me too. Ask anyone here, I don't do anything I don't want to do. I have wanted to fuck you since you stuck your arse in my face," he said, grinning. Unless he was the best actor in NYC, the dark looks he gave me left me without any doubts.

"You're too much." I giggled.

"I'm a man around a pretty woman," he said.

I found myself spontaneously putting my arms around his slim waist and giving him a hug.

He laughed. "Sullivan, you are expressive. Horny, frustrated, sad, and happy all in less than one evening. Your character is turning out to be high maintenance."

"I'd say the same about you," I said, breaking away from him.

He kissed me lightly on the lips. "I admit it."

I shrugged. "Alright, I am too."

He winked at me. "Alright. Next time you are thinking weird, speak up, mood-killer. I'll give you the night off."

I laughed at him. "You're too much."

"One night. You will make it up to my cock," he declared.

"You were going to use your hand. I never agreed to do more," I said.

"So your character's a selfish lover." He scoffed, and we laughed. "I'll eat your pussy so well you will happily suck my cock."

"Do you ever stop?" I joked. A part of me didn't want him to.

"No," he said. "Have you eaten dinner?"

I shook my head. "You?" I glanced down the hall and noticed a small group of partiers nearby.

"I waited for you," he said and took my hand. "I wasn't talking about your pussy again. There's barbeque in the garden."

He placed his hand on my back possessively and the crowd parted to let him get by. I noticed a few lingering looks of curiosity about me. At least the word out there tomorrow would be that the same woman was here, and she wasn't merely a passing fancy. Even though I was one, I reminded myself.

Kayla and Lance were seated at a table and waved us over.

Dylan held a seat out and I sat down.

"Don't move from that seat," he ordered.

I rolled my eyes when he walked away. "You don't have to worry," I called to his back.

He gave me a confused look, then pressed his lips together and moved away.

"Wow, Dylan has gone caveman. I haven't ever seen him behave like that with anyone before," Lance said and chuckled.

"You even got him waiting on you," Kayla mused.

I stared after him and smiled. He was right. The way he was playing it, his friends believed in us. People were falling over to put plates together for him.

"He's great," I said softly and cleared my throat.

"Kayla said it was your first game?" Lance asked.

I nodded.

"Did you see Vandenberg? I mean, what a diver?! He should've been red-carded for what he did today," Lance complained.

We laughed as Lance went on to describe all the instances that he had on record of Vandenberg playing up to the refs. Particularly pointing out every time he had personally bumped against him and he dramatically crumbled on the pitch and wailed.

"He should go into acting, like Dylan," Lance said.

"Who?" Dylan said, placing plates of grilled chicken and potatoes before me.

"Vandenberg," I replied.

"That pathetic wanker," Dylan said, and we all laughed.

Dylan joined in and, even if he was repeating

everything we discussed, we laughed along and I ate the delicious food he brought me.

"You coming to the LA Galaxy game next month? Those matches will be good," Lance asked.

"Yes, she is," Dylan answered for me. "She's my new good luck charm." He winked at me.

"If I don't have to work or have dance classes," I interjected. "We'll talk about schedules," I whispered.

"Yeah," he said. "You do what you need. We'll be there for a week before heading to Seattle, where you can see your family."

The worry on my face must have come through. Dylan touched my chin. "You alright?"

I gave him a small smile. "Of course. Yeah. It would be great. We can invite my parents to the game." We all chatted for a little while more, and slowly people started to leave and the music and dancing had moved to the garden.

Beyoncé's "Runs the World (Girls)" came on and I jumped up. I had learned some of the dance moves in class and got up and started moving as other ladies got up and joined in.

Knox, Tyler, and a few more of the players from the team came out to join Dylan and Lance, as well as a few others I didn't know. The group of us fed off the energy. I fed off the intensely charged stare Dylan had on me. I was so deeply into the music I hadn't even thought about the quick kick and turn I liked to do at the end. The back yard had garden lights, so it wasn't too bright and my skirt wasn't too short. I didn't think it was a big deal. That was until the catcalls from his teammates came out.

Dylan was out of his seat and had his hands around my waist, ushering me out the door to a few disappointed groans and a goodbye from Kayla.

When we reached the sidewalk, he placed me down on my feet. We immediately realized we weren't alone. There was a photog a few houses down with a camera aimed our way. He went into our act. He put on a smile that didn't reach his eyes as he called his driver.

"You like to be on show? No more dancing like that in front of my teammates, or I'll have a problem with them."

"Sorry, I wasn't thinking. I mean, no one saw anything," I stammered.

He pursed his lips but took my hand. "You have on blue lace knickers."

I smiled though my stomach flipped over. "Maybe it's just you looking there," I said with a hint of doubt in my voice.

He snorted. "They were, trust me."

I blew out a breath. Great. Now I was a pantie-flasher.

Dylan put his hands on my shoulders. "You can put your leg behind your head while I'm fucking you, but I don't want them looking at you like that," he said in a low tone.

I forgot how to breathe. I turned away. Damn him. "Stop teasing me. We're not in private."

"Oh, I'm no tease, Brooke, I'm one hell of a promise. So keep those legs closed until I'm ready to open them," he said.

"You're not opening anything," I muttered.

He didn't answer for a few minutes, letting me stew. Then he kissed my lips tenderly, and I smiled adoringly up at him for the cameras. He looked ever the attentive boyfriend as he helped me into the car and we set off.

"I'll be busy, but I expect you to come over on Wednesday for a jog. You'll need to be there at eight a.m. sharp," he said.

"Where do you jog?" I asked.

"Central Park," he said. We were quiet for a few minutes, until he asked, "Do you jog?"

I giggled. "I jog on the treadmill in the gym—"

"You may be in for a surprise," he mused. "But I'll go easy on you." He tucked back the hair that had fallen into my face.

"Yeah, well, I'm not looking to be a sweaty mess on *Page Six*," I said.

His fingers lingered under my chin. "I don't think you could look anything but pretty."

My cheeks warmed, and I fidgeted. "We should get some schedules down and talk about stuff too."

"After the run," he said, firming up our plan. His fingertips trailed down my neck and I shifted in my seat.

"So what do you think of NYC?" I asked.

"I like it but I'll probably eventually move to L.A. I love the feel of the city, but I like the weather and lifestyle there," he said.

"I had once thought about going to Los Angeles, but I had dreams of the Broadway stage. I love everything about acting. As an actor I can be anyone. I have been enjoying doing it since I was a little girl. I used to do it to get attention because my parents were always out working, but, well…" I babbled.

He frowned. "I can sympathize. My dad always

wanted a footballer. He pushed me when I was young. I love football and would have done it anyway. But I sometimes wonder what else I would have done." He blew out a breath and turned his head toward the traffic outside the window.

"Well, now you want to try acting too," I replied.

"Yeah. I do like the idea. It's a good idea... Give me your phone. We should talk during the week, but no stupid videos," he said, changing the subject.

"I'll only send a bunch of cats and dogs," I teased.

"Dogs, maybe." He paused and pulled up a picture of a cute husky pup with his pink tongue hanging out. "That's Rocco."

"Oh, he's so cute," I cooed.

He laughed. "No, he's not cute, he's a tough pain in the butt." He was smiling broadly though.

The driver came around with a pretty gift bag after we got out at my building.

"What's that?" I asked.

"Something you'll need for Wednesday," he said. His lips moved in a sweet slow glide against mine. "I can almost hear you thinking, woman. No one asks to be kissed. They just get kissed."

"What about the begging?" I smirked.

"Mark my words, you'll beg for me to fuck you," he reminded me.

I giggled then lifted on my tiptoes and kissed his lips. "No one asks for a kiss."

He stared after me.

I took the bag and swayed my hips as I walked over to the door and, with a little wave, went inside. He was still there when I closed the door.

I reached the top and immediately turned on the lights and looked out the window. I watched his car move on down the avenue.

Plopping down on the bed, I opened the bag and pulled out a pair of crazy laced-up athletic shoes with a note.

Leave the new sparkly shoes at home

I touched my warm face. *No romance and flowers eh, Dylan?*

But he gave me a pair of athletic shoes with crazy laces, and I swooned because he had been thinking about me. Our relationship may be pretend, but, Dylan Pierce was already getting to me.

CHAPTER

EIGHT

"I still can't believe you are dating Dylan Pierce," Gemma said, bringing in her laptop to show me the pictures she'd seen of us. It was on *Page Six* from the party a couple days ago. If you didn't know me, you'd hardly recognize me. It was a photo capturing the moment where Dylan had carried me outside and placed me down on my feet.

"I swear they find the most unflattering photos they can find," I said, frowning at the wildness of my hair. I emailed a copy of it to myself because Dylan's pout looked sexy and I got to reminisce on all the ways I enjoyed his company. Particularly all the dirty things he had said and the ways he touched my body. He hadn't even really gone too far, but it was intimate. Arousing. Exciting.

"What are you grinning about?" she asked.

I turned my head away and put on my new fancy sneakers. "Nothing… He's really nice."

"Yeah. I'm still surprised at how quickly you did a

one-eighty on him. I don't get why Raymond didn't offer me the promotional spot since you're dating him."

I bit my lip. I hated lying to Gemma, but the only way I could explain how we ended up seeing each other again and not looking for a replacement position for Colby's was to tell her that Dylan chose me for a promotion that night and Raymond had organized it.

"So, when are you going to let him fuck you?" she asked and sat down at the breakfast counter.

I lifted my shoulders. I couldn't...well, shouldn't, but I answered, "We've had one date and I don't want to ruin it," I said.

She laughed at me. "Ruin what? Your dry spell? He's a superstar athlete. He has hundreds of women in the city ready to take your spot. He's gorgeous and has the sexiest most perfect body you may ever get close to, no offense."

I laughed. "None taken." I knew my beauty limits. I was pretty, but I wasn't model-hot.

"But you *do* look extra hot with Dylan." She pointed out another picture of me with Dylan. This one was of us smiling and talking at the match.

I beamed at the picture again. I had been thinking the same thing. As an actress, I was showing that I could act hot. This fake girlfriend role was a good advertisement for casting directors to see me in a different light. Maybe Raymond was right about getting new promotional cards. Besides, Dylan chose me. He didn't seem to think I wasn't pretty enough to get him. "I don't think I should rush it. He always has sex, so making him wait might make me stand out."

"She who waits masturbates," Gemma said, reciting

her sexual motto. "You can be different, but let the man shag you. That's what that man is built for. He's not serious. You get laid and have fun with him. He wants fun. Trust me."

I tilted my head downward. I had judged him just as harshly when I first met him, but after spending a little time in his company, I didn't see Dylan as only sex, though he was sexually alluring and came on stronger than a frat boy at a party. He was hard-working, direct, funny, and charming. "He's not like that all the time. He's different."

"Oh, Brooke. Please don't tell me you are already falling for him." She frowned.

A loud snore came from her bedroom. "Baloo?" I asked.

She shook her head. "Baloo's done. That's West. Baloo wouldn't shave his beard and it scraped my inner thighs too much when he went down on me," she answered bluntly. "You know, stars can be bad in bed. Remember my Chadwick?"

"The plank," I said, and we laughed. Plank was our way of describing a lousy lover. I doubted Dylan would lay there and not put in any effort like Chadwick. I imagined I wouldn't be resting there either. He was like a sergeant, all about command. "Alright. I need to get going."

"Where are you going?" she asked.

"Off to dance and then stagehand training." I did "jazz hands" and she laughed. Then her face turned serious.

"Seriously, you need to be careful with Dylan. Ladies have reported getting loved-up by him and then having him walk away."

"I will," I said and opened the door.

Cinder the cat rushed inside when I opened the door, and this time I left Gemma to chase her out. I made it down the street and to the subway and thought about Dylan up and running through Central Park. Was he thinking of me? Although I had sent several texts and pictures, he responded to only a couple. My last one was of a cute dog on the subway. I had entitled it "Rocco's new pal."

It wasn't until a couple days later that I got a message back from him.

Dylan M. Pierce:Busy with practice. Thank you for the photo. We must reschedule jog for Thursday.

My stomach churned. The message was so generic. It was, however, the dose of reality I needed. When we were together we were pretending, working. We weren't and wouldn't be anything else.

Thursday had arrived and so had my publicity jog with Dylan and I still hadn't heard from him. Still, I dressed in a designer jogging suit, tank top, and sunglasses that picked up the colors in the new shoes he had given me. Placing my hair in a short ponytail, I set off with my calendar in hand in a taxi for Central Park West where Dylan's apartment was located. Because we hadn't been seen together in a couple of days, I hadn't received any additional photographs. However, Raymond had set up some for today.

I found him in his lobby, looking way too good for a morning run, waiting for me. His blond hair was up in a man-bun and his square jaw had a shadow of a beard. His shirt was tight enough to see the perfectly toned ridges of his eight-pack abs. He had shorts that gloriously showed off long muscular thighs and legs. His sneakers were similar to mine.

When our gazes connected, he gave me a smile that didn't reach his eyes, though he brushed his lips against my cheek, causing a tingling with the contact.

"How have you been?" he asked.

"Good. Busy," I said politely.

He placed his hand on the nape of my neck and moved me outside and started stretching. I hadn't noticed the hot sun, and quickly stripped off the jacket, which he took from me. He then handed it to the concierge, along with my bag, after a lingering glance at my breasts in my tank top.

A pap was already waiting and came up to us and asked, "So, Dylan, how long have you two been dating?"

Dylan took my hand and moved us to his waiting car. "Brooke?"

The photographer said my name!

I grinned and waved before we climbed in the car. It was what Raymond had told us to do, to keep them guessing. Hopefully, keep them wanting more of the two of us.

Dylan snorted once we were settled in the car. "That will get old soon," he warned me.

"So since they have the photos, I could go home," I

said, looking out the window.

"No. I thought you wanted to go jogging?" he said and cleared his throat. "We have an away game in Toronto a week from Tuesday. We'll leave on Monday. Can you come?"

I shook my head. "I have stagehand work for an afternoon matinee scheduled that day. It would be too late."

"We are there for five days. I'd like you to be there for at least three," he said.

"I'm not exactly sure, but we can go over our calendars now, if you want," I replied.

His finger traced the shell of my ear and down the side of my neck. "You look pretty. You alright?"

I shivered and smoothed the sides of my hair. "Of course I am." I looked out into traffic.

"You're acting strange," he said.

I glanced at him. *So are you.* "I'm acting." I winked at him.

"Oh." He looked a little hurt. "Well, I prefer you don't. I'd like you relaxed like you were the other day."

"Sorry. I'll work on it," I said and plastered on a smile.

The corners of his mouth turned down, but he didn't push.

Something was wrong, but I didn't know if I should try to get him to tell me what it was. With every glance I stole, I noticed more things that had me worrying over him. His shoulders had dropped, like he had shrunk into himself. He'd turned his head down. His beautiful smile hadn't come back again.

I reached out and took his hand. "Tell me what happened."

He exhaled deeply. "Rocco's sick. I don't know what with, and I can't go home. I don't know if he will be able to come next week."

I covered my mouth. "I'm sorry. I didn't know. I shouldn't have sent that text."

He gave me a weak smile. "You didn't know... It's got me moody."

I reached over and took his hand, and he exhaled. "You can call me anytime you need someone to talk to. I'm sure you have friends, but I'm good at listening."

"Can I call you to fuck too?" he asked. His lip curved slightly upward.

I squinted at him. "I'm being serious."

"So am I," he said.

I wrapped my arms around his side and he pulled me closer. The roadwork had left the car stationary. I meant to give him a hug, but he moved me against his chest into a full-on cuddle. And whatever the man used smelled edible. After a while he asked, "So you want to run or go eat the breakfast I'm making for us?"

I leaned back and gave him a genuine smile. "You cook breakfast?"

"What? Just because I'm incredibly handsome, I can't cook?" he said, his tone light.

I grinned broadly and swatted him, and he grabbed my hand and rubbed the inside with his thumb. "There you are. That's the Brooke I want showing up every time I see her," he said and leaned over to kiss my cheek.

I felt a flutter go through my chest and worked to still it. "So where are we running?" I asked, changing the subject.

"We'll start running in Central Park," he said.

I inched away only to have him tug me back into his arms. "There could be a camera pointing on us now." I doubted it, but I let him put his arm around me and I put my head on his shoulder.

I licked my lips. "Okay. Since we're being friendly again."

He captured my chin and tilted my head up to his striking face. "Tell me."

My pulse sped up, but I pressed on. "I expected to hear from you. It upset me that you didn't return my texts."

His eye contact was firm. "It won't happen again."

The car finally got moving and I allowed myself to re-lax and enjoy the comfort of being with him.

CHAPTER

NINE

Dylan

B rooke was like no one I had met before. She never behaved like she was on a job. I liked that.

I had thoroughly enjoyed her company at the party. She was easygoing. Natural. Funny. Sweet. She was quickly becoming a mate, a friend. That was what I had thought until Tyler had his hand on her. If we didn't have a game, I'd have kicked his arse. He was just as surprised as me.

Usually any single woman was fair game, but it was different with Brooke. We had our public thing going. Maybe I was caught up in the acting, but I couldn't let it go. My dick twitched when she leaned into me. She blushed every time I looked at her. I wanted to see how far down her blush went and watch her come. Fuck. I wasn't supposed to touch her, but I didn't know how I wouldn't. I didn't see why she couldn't be my friend with benefits.

The way she had trembled and moaned when I touched her clit through her skirt, told me that she wanted me just as much. It took all the control I had not to pull it up, slip my hands in her panties and feel her pussy. But I knew I wasn't going to stop if I did. And she wasn't ready for me. I knew she wanted me to, but she was scared. She told me she wanted sex to mean something. The warning bells went off at that. But not enough to stop me from wanting to fuck her.

She had a wild streak too. That kick she did at the party had become the brunt of jokes with my teammates. It had me threatening every one of them not to fuck with her or me. I liked it too.

What I liked most about being around her was that she didn't put on airs. She was normal. She was also grateful. I'd bought women plenty of gifts way more expensive than a pair of shoes. The more I gave the more they looked to take, but not Brooke. She acted like those shoes were made of diamonds. It was like it was a big deal for her. Though Raymond said she came from money. I didn't understand that.

She sent a dozen texts of photos of her in those shoes, doing silly dance moves. I enjoyed each one thoroughly, especially the way she smiled in them. Each one had me thinking of her. I wanted to tell her that, but I didn't want to give her the wrong idea. We were only going to be around each other for a short time. I wasn't looking for more than that. I had my goals, and she had hers too. So I left it.

Then Mum phoned and said Rocco was sick. I couldn't lose my buddy. I loved that dog. To most he was just a dog, but to me that dog was everything. His being sick threw me off my game. I wanted to get on a plane home.

I struggled to get through my routine of practice and training the last couple days. I didn't need any distractions, and that included Brooke. But now, seeing the way Brooke cared affected me. She was pissed I disappeared, but when she found out, she forgave me.

She put no pressure on me. I wanted to keep that for as long as I could. Eventually, she would and I'd have to move on. But that didn't mean we couldn't enjoy each other.

I wasn't ready for a real relationship. We were not in a real relationship. That was the whole reason I agreed to do this in the first place. But hanging out with her was alright.

The driver pulled up, and we got out.

"Come here and let me stretch you." I smiled to myself. She looked like she wasn't going to. She didn't like me ordering her around. But she came over and we sat on the ground with our feet touching and I took her hands and pulled her toward me. Bending over, I could see the swell of her round tits in her tank top. It was tight enough to see her nipples poking out in a way that made my cock stir. It was turning me on, but the fucking cameras would pick it up. I let go and helped her up to stand. She trembled at my touch on her hips.

"Fix your top," I whispered.

Her brows lowered before she tilted her head down and there appeared that blush of hers that made my balls ache. She made it worse this time by sucking on her bottom lip. I had to force my eyes away and think of something annoying to calm my dick down. When I turned back, she had a little smile on her face. She enjoyed teasing my cock. We'd both enjoy it more if I could get her to suck it. If I could fuck her. Shit. If I kept this up, my cock sticking out of my shorts would be on film.

I tore my gaze away from her and jogged in place. She followed me, but even with that sports-bra she had on, her tits bounced. Fuck.

I took a deep breath and said, "Stay as close to my side as possible. You stop, I stop with you. Got it?"

"I got it," she agreed.

My driver handed us waters, and we set off on the paved path. The park was busier than I was used to since we had gotten a later start, but I still took her on my normal route. She kept my pace but stopped at her fancy. First, it was the Alice in Wonderland statue. Then to admire the roller skaters. Next a guy with a guitar and John Lennon puppet. When she got me to stop again for a cute husky she thought looked a little like Rocco, I was done.

"Now I know why you go to the gym," I complained.

"We paused a little. We can go a few more miles," she said.

I cocked a brow, "Can we now? No I'll finish up in the gym. We'll go back to my place."

Thing was, I didn't take women back to mine to do more than fuck and send home. However, I had found a place that delivered proper British groceries and ordered some to make a proper fry-up of rashers, sausage, beans, and eggs. Brooke didn't fuss over food at the party. So I thought she'd like it. We had to get stuff sorted, anyway. I wanted her at my games.

She followed me as we ran back to the car. We were both sweaty. I ran her more than I had intended. I was sure I saw a photographer taking pictures. But I didn't care and she shouldn't either. Her hair was damp and curled at her hair line. Her eyes were darting around and she had on that blush she got when I stared at her.

She looked beautiful.

CHAPTER

TEN

Brooke

U pon returning to Dylan's building, we breezed by the paparazzi and went straight up to his apartment near the top.

Once he put in his passcode, he held the door for me to walk inside. The place was a modern open-plan layout with massive floor-to-ceiling windows, dark wood flooring, and a large fireplace built into the wall. The place was decorated with long modular couches with perfectly matched tables and chairs. The fixtures were stone and steel. The kitchen was chrome and dark wood. Nothing in the place appeared personal or warm, as I was beginning to think of him. All except for the large doggie bed, bowl, and chew toys left out for his dog, Rocco.

Removing my shoes, I padded over and picked up one of the brightly colored toys. "You got it all set up for him."

Dylan called out from the kitchen. "Yeah. He will need new toys. I'm not sure what my parents will send along with him."

"Can I help?" I asked, walking up and watching him put bacon in the oven and heat up beans. "You're fine."

"I'm going to have a shower." He pointed to a hall behind him. "There is a guest room I left open so you can shower too."

I chewed on my lip. "I didn't bring anything to change into."

"Just pull a shirt out of the closet," he replied.

"And shorts?" I added.

He pretended not to hear me until I tut-tutted, then said, "My shorts are in the drawer, but they won't fit you."

I pursed my lips. "I'm not sitting dressed only in a T-shirt."

His bedroom was open and I could see a large platform bed and window before I turned into the guest room. I found T-shirts where he claimed and removed one of his New York Football Club shirts that smelled of fresh linen. I went toward the tile-and-glass shower, and quickly stripped down and got in. He had a line of products in there and I spent extra time trying every shampoo and conditioner he had. Dylan was a bit of a metrosexual. Then again, maybe women slept over and this was their bathroom. A weirdness went through me. It was in here or in there with him, and I doubted I'd get out of there without him touching me. He was being good.

I dried myself and brushed my hair. The shirt hung to my knees, but the shorts were too big and kept slipping down my hips. It took me a good ten minutes to tie them both in a silly knot to keep them in place, but it didn't appear flattering, which had me trying to fix them over and again. Finally, I gave up on pretty and tied them as best I could, then hurried into the kitchen where Dylan was. He had finished cooking the food and was stacking the dishwasher. His damp hair was swept up to the crown of his head. He looked smoking hot in the tank and shorts he had changed into.

He turned to me and laughed. "You're looking mighty fine, Ms. Sullivan."

I giggled. "I look ridiculous, but I didn't bring extra clothing, Mr. Pierce."

Sullivan, I'm Starling. Sullivan was my public last name. We hadn't gone over our backgrounds previously, but this was as good as any place to start.

I sighed and sat on the barstool at the island. "I don't know if Raymond told you, but I'm Brooke Starling. Allister Starling's daughter."

He gave me a blank look. So I told him all about my father's financial success.

"If your father has all that, then why doesn't he help you out?" he asked.

I jutted my chin. "That's not the Starling way. He had to earn his way and his father before him. He willed everything to businesses and trusts. In fact, none of his money will be mine. So it's best I find my own way as he and his father did in life."

Dylan's brows furrowed. "He sounds like a right arsehole. I'd never do that. My father didn't have much, but he'd give the shirt off his back. My mum too. They had jobs, but the second I needed them, they were there to help me out. They helped me make a career in football. Your father should help you, too." He fixed our plates and served them.

My stomach churned. *He'd be more proud of me if I did it on my own.* "I chose acting, and he doesn't know how to help me with that."

Dylan scoffed. "He could figure it out. My parents didn't know everything about getting me into football, but they worked at it," Dylan said. He wasn't giving my father an inch. It was admirable, but I didn't want to paint my father in a negative light.

"I don't want his help. I want to do it myself—well, you're helping me," I said.

"We're helping each other," he corrected me.

I licked my lips. "If it gets too hard my dad loans me—"

"Loan?! He makes his daughter take a loan? He can fuck off," he growled.

I paused between bites. "Hey, that's my dad."

Dylan tightened his jaw and said, "Who's behaving like a bastard. I can't stand anyone that places conditions on those they are supposed to care about. You see need, you solve it. There are enough hard lessons in life." He ate, and we didn't talk for a while.

After we finished our breakfast, I finally broke the silence by saying, "He's not that bad. I'm sorry I painted a poor picture of him. He can be good to me. He made me stronger, and it's what is needed for this business. I'm okay."

He sighed. "Fine. I'm sorry I upset you. But if you were mine, I wouldn't ask for your permission. I would help and you would take it."

I smiled inwardly. He meant well. He was a good man. "Thank you and thank you for breakfast. It was delicious."

"Tell me about your mum?" he asked.

"Mom's great. She sells Mary Kay and has a party shop she runs," I replied.

"Mum likes parties. She throws parties for all the kids in our neighborhood that can't afford them," he replied.

My insides warmed. "Your mom sounds wonderful."

He grinned. "She is. All of my family is. They were like a family to everyone." He poured me a glass of orange juice.

I frowned. *Not just him.* "That must've been hard."

He sighed. "It was, but it taught me not to be selfish. It kept me grounded."

"That's a positive outlook. I acted out to get attention, and you were a good boy," I teased.

He chuckled. "I wasn't good. I raised hell and had my fun. Still have my fun, but that's part of growing up. Thing is, I have been playing football for twenty-four years. Twelve years professionally. I had a lot of away games and training growing up. I got used to being independent. I'm not perfect, but it all turned out alright."

"Is it hard to be away from Manchester City?" I asked, finishing off my drink.

"Yeah. I do miss the team, but that's the life of sports. You can't do it forever," he said. "Unlike acting."

I inhaled. "If you're lucky."

He softened. "It will happen. You stick with your

goal. That's what I did."

I lowered my head and smiled as warmth filled my chest. *He pep-talks!*

"You succeeded bringing your team back to the Premier League," I enthused.

He gave me a broad smile. "You googling me?"

"Maybe," I teased. He poked me in the side, and I giggled.

My phone buzzed with an incoming text message. It was from Raymond.

Ray. WTS: Rent wants to test you out by having you join the cast as an alternate in their ensemble.

I screamed in excitement. It was an older show, but plenty of now famous actors started in this show and went on to international stardom. I had been given a chance, all because of Dylan.

He rushed over to my side. "What is it?"

I beamed. "*Rent*, the musical I'm doing the stagehand stuff for, said they'd let me perform in their matinee!"

"When?" he asked.

I sent Raymond a message and got back a reply.

Ray. WTS: A week from Sunday!

I scrunched up my face. "You won't be able to come, will you?"

"I'll make it happen before I leave for Toronto," he said to me.

I jumped up into his arms. He was as happy as me.

He let out a chuckle and lifted me by my ass as I tightened my hands around his neck. "This means a lot to me. I know it's just…"

"No. Remember, I only do what I want to do," he said. "I want to be there and see you."

"I might be able to go to the first game in Toronto and come back," I said.

I squeezed him tight, then pulled back and planted a big kiss on his lips. I meant to make it one of those happy celebratory kisses of a hard peck and a few cheers, then break apart and jump in place. But this was Dylan. Nothing since I met him went exactly as planned. He took over. His kiss had tantalizing persuasion that had me returning it back with reckless abandon, our tongues massaging each other's, our bodies holding on tight.

When we sought to catch our breath, he swung me around and placed me down on my feet, and when he did, my shorts had fallen down. The shirt was still tied up in front, exposing me from the waist down.

Our gazes locked and my mind went into a tailspin. My whole body heated with lust and embarrassment. I couldn't bring myself to speak as the air thickened between us.

I swiftly turned away and desperately sought to untie the shirt.

But Dylan's hands took my waist, turning me around "You have nothing to be embarrassed about. You are happy and you are beautiful." He dropped down to his knees and placed his hands on my hips before pressing a kiss against the top of my bare mound and steadying me as I trembled in his large hands. "Tell me what you want and it's yours."

I closed my eyes against the intensity of the moment. My heartbeat sped up. "You make it sound so simple," I rasped.

"It is. I promise," he said. He tugged the knot loose on the shirt. "Now open your eyes and tell me the truth."

I took a breath and said, "I want you to have sex with me." My voice held an edge to it. I was upset with my willingness to mess up what was going right, for twenty minutes of pleasure.

"We are not ruining anything," he said, as if he lifted the thought from my head.

"This is us. Sex could make us more natural together." He obviously gave this some thought. But he wasn't backing down. He had said it was inevitable. I was doing this, or actually letting him do me. His hand lifted my shirt up enough to stare at my pussy, which was becoming wetter by the second.

"I get tested monthly. I'm clean. I use condoms too. You on the pill?" he asked.

I licked my lips. This was all really happening. "Implant… I'm clean."

He took my hands. "Look at me."

I blinked up at him and my breath hitched. He was blatant in his lust and need. Was it for me? I didn't dare ask.

He pressed his lips at the pulse at my wrist. "I know you're scared, but you don't need to be. I'll go easy on you our first time. I'll take care of you."

I cast my gaze down as a flutter went through my chest. This was not going as I had expected. I thought he'd have me against the wall by now, fucking me senseless. Instead, he gives me words that exposed a deep place of need inside me. It was more of a sweet, intimate promise from a lover to someone special than from a man wanting causal sex.

Was this the way he did all of his women? In a way it was not only dangerous, it was cruel. I tugged my shirt back in place and moved out of his grasp.

I pressed my lips together. "You shouldn't say you 'care' when you don't. Is this because of what I told you about how things are in my family? I didn't tell you for sympathy... I can't do this now."

I rushed off toward the spare bedroom, with Dylan on my heels, following me.

He grabbed my shoulders and turned me around. "You want me to treat you like a bastard, Brooke? I won't do it. You don't control how I fuck you."

I glared at him. There was the cocky bastard side of Dylan. He wasn't aware of what he was doing that was bothering me, so I told him. "Fucking wasn't the problem, it's...saying you care. You don't really know me."

"So? I have to know you to care enough to make you feel good? That's silly," he said. "I could fuck you and send you out, but I don't think that will work or keep things going with our deal."

I blew out my breath. He had a point. This wasn't about sentiments. This was about maintaining our pretend relationship and having sex. I was still here, and I didn't want to leave tension between us. "I see. I misunderstood. Sorry."

"High maintenance," he grumbled, but his eyes were glittering.

I wrapped my legs around him as he lifted me in his arms.

"I'm wet for you," I mumbled and buried my head in his neck and breathed in his fresh scent.

"I know you are and I will take care of you." He took me to his bedroom and lightly kicked the door shut behind us then placed me down on my feet. "Now, take off your shirt, get on the bed and spread your legs for me," he commanded.

My mind wanted to tell him not to order me around, but my pussy clenched in anticipation of what Dylan would do with me. I wasn't body conscious, but I'd never been with a man as good-looking or experienced as Dylan before. I hesitated a second, but still dutifully pulled off my shirt and lay on the bed, spreading my legs open for him.

Dylan took off his tank top, revealing an uninterrupted view of his insanely hot, ripped, tanned, muscular body and abs. He left on his shorts as he moved closer to the bed and sucked in his breath.

"You blush down to your pussy," he said, his voice deep with lust.

I covered my face. "I'm trying not to."

"But you know I like it."

"Is that why I do it?" I grinned at his conceit.

He grinned back. "Your body wants to please me." He stalked over to the bed like he was setting out to prove it. His hands gripped my thighs and pulled me down to the edge where he stared down at me and groaned. "You fought with me and you're dripping wet." He grunted as he rubbed a finger against my swollen, aching clit.

I shuddered and moaned, lifting my hips up for more pressure.

He pressed me back down and kissed the inside of my thigh. "Relax, Brooke. I've got you."

I wanted to lay back and enjoy. I also wanted to watch what he'd do to me.

Before I could say another thing, his tongue pressed in and slid through my soft flesh as he opened my legs wider. "Fuck, Brooke, your pussy tastes so sweet."

"Dylan," I moaned as I arched my back, gripping the sheet below me. My thighs trembled under his powerful grasp and I got hotter as his tongue ran back and forth, up and down my pussy.

"Mmm...you've got a hot, juicy pussy begging to be sucked," he said with a growl.

Dylan moaned against me as he closed his full sexy lips around my clit and gently sucked.

I came, crying out as pleasure filled me. I covered my face with my hands. He had barely started, and I came so quickly. "That felt good," I mumbled

He grinned up at me. "You coming was sexy as fuck, but I'm not done with you."

Dylan moved my legs to his shoulders and kept me firmly in his powerful grasp. He started again, with long, deep caresses and strokes of his tongue through my slick folds, reigniting the electrical sparks of the aftershocks. I quivered hard under the intensity. This was unforeseen territory for me.

He added his finger inside me and started stroking

and swirling his tongue over my clit again, building me back up to another orgasm.

"Ohhhhh...Dylan," I said and moaned.

"You've got a tight pussy. You're going to squeeze my big cock when I fuck you." He pumped two fingers in as his tongue lapped and licked my clit, and I exploded, convulsing hard against his mouth. He grunted and kept on licking me.

"Dylan, I can't come again," I said hoarsely.

He kissed my thigh. "You will."

I was tired but turned on by his demand. I could feel the need rising again with every stroke of his tongue on me. I found myself lifting up for more.

"Grab my head, Brooke, put me where you need me."

My hand reached down and grabbed a handful of his thick hair as he gently continued to lick me. The sensation was overwhelming and I shook hard against him.

He penetrated me with his tongue as his fingers thrust in and out of my pussy.

My heart pounded in my ears and my whole body went ridged, as I broke apart.

Dylan let me hold on to his head as I shattered under him, and when I came down, he finally released me. My limbs felt heavy as he moved me over and kissed up my hip and up to my breasts until he had my face in his hands. I couldn't imagine what he must have seen. My skin felt hot, my eyes heavy and watery.

I said the first thing that came to my mind and what I knew he would appreciate. "Dylan, let me suck your cock. Please."

He let out a deep, sexy laugh. "You rest for a minute,

then bring that sweet, tight pussy to my mouth and I'll let you suck my cock."

He rubbed the side of my face, his gaze softening. "You coming for me was the sexiest thing I have ever seen."

"You say that to all the ladies," I joked.

"No, I don't," he said. His expression serious. "I enjoyed pleasuring you."

"And I loved being pleasured by you. It was more than I imagined." I clamped my hand over my mouth.

He pulled my hand away and kissed me lightly on the lips. "Same for me. I've been thinking about how good it would be to eat your pussy and fuck you, since we met."

My face burned. "You haven't fucked me yet."

He grinned wickedly. "I will. You can start by sucking my cock," he instructed and pulled off his shorts. His cock was thick and rigid with pre-cum beaded at the tip.

I moved down his incredible body and reached for his shaft, which felt velvety soft to the touch, and gripped the base and squeezed.

He pulsed under my grip, and I moaned, enjoying the groan he let out. His hands grabbed a handful of my hair as I closed around the head of his cock and sucked. "Take me deeper," he said, growling out his command.

I felt myself get wetter as I let him feed his cock in, inch by inch, breathing in through my nose and inhaling his clean, masculine scent that was all Dylan. He moaned and gripped my head tighter until his cock reached the back of my throat and I gagged. He slid his shaft over my tongue, then rocked his hips gently forward, his cock moving deeper inside my mouth, forcing me to swallow around him.

"Yes," he hissed. "Fuck, Brooke, suck me like that."

A chime sound went off in the apartment. I kept sucking until the sound came again.

"Wait," he instructed. Dylan stopped moving and eased his cock from my mouth. His brows furrowed as he snatched a remote and pressed a button and a TV I hadn't noticed came on. "What the fuck is this?"

I frowned, until I saw the image on the screen. It was Salvatore standing by the door with a beautiful brunette who looked vaguely familiar.

"Who is she?" I asked him.

He sighed heavily. "Nicola. She's my lawyer. She was my longest month relationship."

CHAPTER
ELEVEN

Salvatore and his lawyer ex-girlfriend? Neither one could find us naked in bed.

"I'll jump in the shower. You'll need to answer the door," Dylan said, moving over toward the bathroom.

I rushed up behind him. "I can't do that. I mean, why can't you?" I said. My voice was shrill.

I followed his gaze down to his hard cock, and my breath hitched. Damn, was he hot. "Oh, right."

"Keep staring at my cock like that and I'll forget them and fuck you."

"Just get in the shower," I replied.

He chuckled despite it all and turned on the shower.

I touched my warm cheeks. "Everything we did together is written all over my face." I splashed my cheeks with cold water. "What am I going to say?"

"You came over for the run and we discussed schedules," he called out. "But hurry."

I looked frantically around for my clothes and

remembered they were in the spare room, and quickly changed into everything but my panties, which I sought to put in my purse but couldn't find. Rushing back into the living room, I tucked the shorts he gave me into the couch cushion. Then I took a couple of cleansing breaths and caught my reflection in the mirror near the door. *I'm a woman with a crush on an athlete, not a woman who just had three mind-blowing orgasms on his face.*

Damn. I hadn't even gotten the chance to savor our experience or even touch all of his magnificent body.

"There," I murmured to myself. Now my reflection held something I could work with. I drew on the feeling of the unrequited groping to cover the post-orgasm bliss on my face. The bell rang again.

I smoothed my hair in place and called out, "I'll be right there."

"Brooke?" Salvatore's brows rose as I opened the door.

The brunette stepped around him and eyed me coolly before thrusting out her hand to shake. "Nicola Spencer, Dylan's lawyer." She had a trace of a British accent. "I hadn't arrived in time to see your show at Colby's."

"Nice to meet you," I said in a polite tone.

"I wasn't expecting to find you here," Salvatore said after closing the door and moving to the living room.

"We just got back from our run..." I started and stopped, flicking my gaze at the woman.

"She's aware of everything and has a non-disclosure," he assured.

"Where is Dylan?" she asked.

"He went to take a shower," I said nonchalantly and opened my calendar.

She walked on back toward his bedroom.

"He's coming out—" I said, my voice trailing off. I turned to Salvatore. "Will he get upset by her going back there?"

Salvatore smiled and shook his head. "Leave her. She's actually here to solve one of our little problems. Ray and I discussed how it would be hard for Dylan to be left without...sexual company." He glanced over his shoulder. "Since the two of them are still friends, she would work out perfectly."

I put on a smile and feigned a sigh of relief while my stomach muscles twisted. "That would work out for the best."

"Yes, for all of us," he said and patted my hand. "The press and the public are falling in love with your relationship one photo at a time."

"I hope so," I said and glanced over at the hall. "Do you think Dylan will agree to it?"

"Of course he will," Salvatore said.

A loud high-pitched laugh erupted. "I'd say he's agreeing right now."

"That's great..." I cleared my throat. "Would you please tell me more about Dylan's schedule? We were exchanging family histories after the run, and we only got as far as the Toronto game."

Salvatore went on to fill me in on their dates for their games for the next five weeks, and I listened and chatted along while my mind was back there with Dylan and Nicola. Every minute she was back there with him had me beating myself up at my stupidity. Yes, we weren't together, but our sexual contact had complicated things for me.

I was already upset. How was I supposed to handle seeing him intimate with her now?

"Salvatore. You didn't call. I don't allow stop-ins," Dylan said crossly as he finally came out and joined us. He was wearing a shirt and jeans. That was about as far as I allowed myself to look at him. I couldn't look at his face yet. He'd know that I was upset and everything would be messed up, but when I caught Nicola's beaming expression, I realized I didn't need to.

"Sorry," Salvatore said. "I was meeting with Nicola about some of your trust agreements when a charity opportunity came in. We think it would be perfect, actually, for you and Brooke."

Nicola's smile wilted a little.

I glimpsed at Dylan as he stopped next to her, his hand now casually placed on her shoulder. "We can discuss it later. After Brooke leaves," he responded.

My heart dropped to my feet. I was being dismissed. I turned back to Salvatore. "Dylan's right. I should be going."

"Why not now?" Nicola chimed in. They came over and sat down across from me and Salvatore. "Steve Westcott, the designer of the century, is doing a charity runway show for The New York City Fashion Foundation for Children and Families in Need. They have created an athletic line and the proceeds will go exclusively to the charity. They want Dylan to walk in their show in Bryant Park."

"I think it would be a great idea if you came as support," Salvatore said.

My jaw dropped open. "That is wonderful news," I

said enthusiastically. "I'd love to go. When is it?"

"Next Sunday," Dylan answered for him. "Nicola just told me."

"Oh, I have a prior commitment. I won't be able to attend, then," I said and hunched my shoulders.

"I'm sorry I won't be able to go to your performance," Dylan said, his voice dropping an octave.

I swallowed. "No worries… It's nothing."

"If there is a conflict with your schedule, I can talk to Raymond and see if the show could get a substitute for that night," Salvatore offered.

"No," Dylan said. "Nicola can go with me." He placed his arm along the back of her seat.

Salvatore and Nicola grinned at each other.

"Then it's all settled," she said.

I gathered up my things. "I need to go. I have a lot to prepare for."

"I can give you a ride home," Salvatore said.

"I can…we can give her a ride down to Nicola's office," Dylan said to Nicola.

"My office at my *home* in the West Village," she explained, her eyes glittering. "How far away are you from the West Village?"

I bent down and tried to lace up my new sneakers "I'm all the way in the uncharted land of East Village," I half-joked. "I think I want to run."

Dylan's hands appeared next to my own, and he took the laces away and tied them up. "Smartarse," he said under his breath.

"I got it," I said.

"You're making a mess of it," he said. "You'll take the

ride home."

"No, I won't," I said forcefully and recovered with a laugh. "I'm a big girl. I ride the subway."

He laid his hands on top of my feet and gently squeezed. "All done."

My pulse increased as I looked down at them, my mind journeying to his warm hands, holding and caressing me, but now that was over. It could no longer be. "And on to the next one," I softly snipped.

"Brooke," Dylan said and reached for my foot again, but I quickly stood and moved back from him. "I'm going to finish my exercise," I announced, and glanced at the clouds through one of the large windows, "before it rains."

"Salvatore, take Brooke home," Dylan instructed.

He laughed at us. "You two are great together."

"We should get going. Dylan agreed to dinner," Nicola said to Dylan.

"Nice to meet you. Thank you, Salvatore, for the information," I said, then turned to Dylan, hoping he couldn't see my trembling lip. "Thanks for the run and breakfast."

"You're welcome," he said and grinned.

He opened the door and, after a quick wave, I rushed forward and down the hall.

"Brooke, wait. Damn it," Dylan called out.

"Have fun. I'll see you in Toronto," I said and did my cutesy twirl before taking the stairs. I didn't stop until I had reached the outside and broke into a run. I ran down the avenue for a few blocks until I found what I had always looked for—that safe place to collect myself. That safe place to stop.

Sitting down on a bench at a bus stop, I put my face in my hands as my mind struggled to come to grips with all that had happened between me and Dylan. I had easily exposed myself in his bed, only to let him easily cast me aside for Nicola. I scolded myself. I wiped the drips of tears from the leather case of my calendar and took a deep breath. No matter how much I was beginning to like him, he didn't think of me the same way.

Dylan Pierce was a hard lesson to learn, but one I wouldn't forget.

My subway ride back to the East Village gave me a chance to put everything in perspective. I enjoyed what I let Dylan do to me, but I shouldn't have thought it meant anything. We were considering being friends with benefits. But what became clear was that I wasn't someone who could do that with him.

I supposed Dylan had a reputation to live up to and what he did to me was amazing, but way too personal, too intimate. My past lovers never carried me to bed, or talked dirty to me. None of them gave me multiple amazing orgasms. Maybe that was how he was with all his women and it's no wonder why they were upset. It was wrong to make a partner think you cared just to make your sexual experience better.

I couldn't accept that treatment, but Nicola obviously could and was clearly willing to go back to him. Perhaps she was a perfect solution. She appeared to have no qualms about being his private lover while I remained his public. I had time to get myself together before Toronto. I'd keep up our public charade, and stay away from him in private. He should be with her, and focus on his acting and charity work. And I'd keep my focus on my acting and my opportunity to be on stage in a show.

I was going to be in the show *Rent!* It was the first show I had gone to see when I came to New York City, and I enjoyed working behind the scenes but wanted more than anything to join the cast. While I was troubled by what happened with Dylan, I was happy and grateful for what was happening with my career. It was a step away from odd jobs. It was a chance.

In fact, I was feeling a little better by the time I reached home, though Dylan remained not too far from my mind. He was insanely hot. He was arrogant, dirty, and opinionated, but he was also kind, funny, and sweet. But even with all that, I liked him. What was I going to do?

I mulled over our situation as I took a shower and ate dinner. While I was going over the script, my phone buzzed with a text message. It was from Dylan.

Dylan M. Pierce: We should talk.

I looked at the ceiling.

Brooke. S.: We have nothing to talk about. It's fine. I promise you.

Dylan M. Pierce: I don't believe you. I'll come over.

I frowned down at the phone and wrote back:

Brooke. S.: I'm probably going to bed.

Dylan M. Pierce: Then I should come over.

I quickly wrote back:

Brooke. S.: No. I don't think that's a good idea. Thank you for the afternoon.

Dylan M. Pierce: What the fuck are you thanking me for?

Brooke. S.: For spending time with me. It was great! I'll see you in Toronto.

I sighed and waited for a few minutes. He didn't write back, and I put my phone away. I went to my bed and curled up in a ball and fell asleep.

When I awoke a while later, the place was lit. I moved the room divider aside, and I found Gemma ironing a pair of jeans.

"You going out?" I asked the obvious.

"Yeah. A group of us are going to a movie," she replied.

"Can I tag along?" I asked.

She gave me an odd look. "Of course. You don't have to ask. West, Frieda, and Baloo should be here soon."

"Baloo with West?" I called over my shoulder as I went over to my closet.

"They get on," she called back.

I shook my head. How Gemma could casually go out with guys she had sex with was beyond me. I found a summer dress and put it on. I trimmed my bangs a little and grabbed a scarf and sandals before heading back into the room.

"So I have news!" I said and told her about *Rent*. She jumped up and down with me.

"We will have to celebrate. Call Dylan and we can go out and party," she said.

I glanced down at my shoes. "He's busy tonight."

"Something happen?" she asked.

I rubbed the space between my brow. "Yes. No. It's just, you know…new."

"You all loved-up yet?" she teased.

"Hardly," I said and told her about the oral sex, leaving out Nicola.

"Three orgasms? He's an overachiever. That's a sexual goldmine," she said. "Take the ride until he's ready to let you off."

I blew out a breath. "If only it was that easy."

"It is if you'd let it be," she said. Our door buzzed. "Don't be dramatic, Brooke."

I narrowed my eyes. "Hey? Why would you accuse me of being the problem?" I went over and opened the door and my heart jumped in my throat. Dylan stood there, surrounded by our group of friends who were grinning up at him. His energy and allure instantly filled the space. As always, he looked good. His eyes bore down on me and the air crackled between us. I took in a ragged breath and shifted on my feet.

"Aren't you going to introduce us around?" Gemma prodded.

"We met in the hallway," Dylan said, which Frieda, Baloo, and West echoed sheepishly.

He shook Gemma's hand perfunctorily, but right after he did, he came to stand close to me. His hand was warm as he closed it around my nape. His lips brushed my ear as he whispered, "We need to talk."

My eyelids fluttered. "This isn't a good time," I whispered.

I tilted my head to our friends who stood there gawking like they had front row seats to a nighttime reality TV show. I was no better in keeping my composure. Dylan didn't seem to care and moved even closer to me.

I took a step away from him. "We're going to see a movie. I don't want to hold up everyone," I said, my tone light.

"I won't keep you long," he replied, pressing himself against my side. He trailed his hand down my spine to settle right above the swell of my buttocks.

I inhaled noisily, and he softly laughed. Damn him. I couldn't move away from him without causing a scene and he knew it. Therefore, I did the only thing that came to mind. I let out a little laugh and lifted my brows at Gemma for help.

"Alright. We are off," she said, taking my hint. "You know what we are seeing. Maybe Dylan can drop you off."

"We can go downstairs and wait or you can join us," Baloo spoke up.

"He can't," I said with disappointment in my tone.

He sighed. "She's right, I can't."

They all surged forward and shook his hand before leaving.

"Do come by again," Gemma mused, her facial expression suggestive before closing the door firmly behind her. Once the door was closed I turned around and asked, "What are you doing here?"

"So this is where you live," Dylan said reprovingly as he moved us to sit on the couch. "Have your parents seen your apartment?"

I folded my arms. "Yeah. They have visited, but I'm sure you didn't come over to insult our place. Why are you here? I thought you were going to Nicola's." I tried and failed to disguise the contempt in my voice.

His brows lowered. "You're in a mood. I knew it."

I jutted my chin. "So are you."

He sighed. "Listen, Nicola and I are old friends. Her office is in her home. I didn't know about their idea—"

"Salvatore filled me in," I cut him off. "I think it's a great idea."

He cocked a brow. "Is that so?"

I pursed my lips. "Yes. I suppose you have history together."

"Yes and that's why making her a fuck-buddy would make it more complicated," he explained. He moved closer and placed his hand on my thigh. A tremor went through me at his contact.

My heartbeat quickened. "It's complicated, but you're not saying no..." I bit the inside of my cheek to cover my annoyance. "I guess it's something you're considering."

He glanced at me, and I looked away and folded my arms.

"I don't want Nicola in my bed, I want you." He slid his hand along my bare thigh and over to the top of my panties and stroked my slit through the fabric. "I only got a taste of your pussy today, and that's not enough." He let out a groan when he discovered I was wet.

I closed my thighs around his hand. "We can't."

"Why not?" he murmured, wiggling his fingers deeper between my thighs, and I gasped as his deft fingers slipped around the lace to stroke against my pulsing clit. A moan escaped my lips. He grunted. "You're hot and needy. Any time you need me to touch you, you come to me." He crooked his finger and massaged a place that had me arching up and opening my legs wider to give him more access, and he took it. His thumb pressed and rubbed against my swollen clit.

I closed my eyes. "Dylan, think about this."

"What is there to think about?" he purred. "We want each other. You relax and let go. I'll make you come all night... Let me take care of you."

I pushed him hard and scooted away from him on the couch. There was that word again, "care." "No. I don't want to do this with you. I can't be your fuck-buddy."

"Why? You haven't even tried," he said in frustration. "If you're worried about our public persona, we can manage. We will be careful."

I licked my lips. He wasn't getting it. "Look at me, Dylan." I let my guard down and let my face show how truly affected I was by what happened between us today. "Sure, I can act, but I'm not good when it comes to reality. We need to work together."

He sat back and studied me as silence fell between us.

I finally said, "I can still do our public agreement. I don't want to lose the job. You do what works for you, and if it's Nicola,"—I grimaced—"I understand."

"Oh, you do, do you?" He folded his arms.

I pursed my mouth. "Yeah and I'll do the same."

His eyes flashed at me. "What the fuck is 'I'll do the same' supposed to mean?"

I shrugged. "I have a friend with benefits too. I'll use him and you can have Nicola in private."

"Who are you willing to let fuck you and pass me over for?" he asked indignantly.

"If you need to know, his name is Collin Baxter—"

"Collin?" He let out a derisive laugh. "You are going to let a Collin fuck you instead of me? A 'Collin' wouldn't know what to do with you."

I glared at him. "You are judging him by his name. You don't even know him."

"I don't have to know," he said. "I bet he asked you if you orgasm. I bet he doesn't even try to make you come if he doesn't."

My face burned. I wanted to deny it, but he was right. "It's not all about fucking with me. He's gentle—"

"I was gentle when I sucked your pussy," he said.

My core tightened in response to his crass words as I was instantly brought back to the luxurious sensation of every stroke and suction of his tongue. I lowered my eyelids as I worked to regain control of my breathing. All under Dylan's fierce gaze glaring across at me. Damn him. "That's not the point. You threw that back in my face because I tell you that things can't work between us."

"No, Brooke. I've got a right to fucking defend myself

when you're comparing me with an inept wanker. I know you want me—"

"This isn't about what I want or what we did together," I said, cutting him off. "It's about bringing professionalism back to our relationship. This afternoon was a mistake." He reached over and clasped my shoulders. My skin broke out in goosebumps at the electricity of his touch. His jaw was tense. "It wasn't a mistake. You want to push for more when you haven't put in the time to get it."

My lips parted. "That's not true. I don't want to get hurt. I still want us to be friends... I like you," I stammered.

He sneered. "Friends? Now, how would that be fair to me when I want to fuck you every time I look at you? We can't be friends. We can be work colleagues and keep our public relationship. That's all."

I looked down at my hands that were unsteady on my knees. I didn't like the idea of only seeing Dylan in public, but he was right. I had no idea how I could be his friend after what we did together this afternoon. Therefore, all I could do was agree. "Alright. If that's what you want."

"No, it's not what I want." His hand covered one of my own and a shiver of awareness went through me. His closeness was so bracing. He raised goosebumps along my skin as he moved his hand higher up my skirt. "You want me, Brooke, I can feel it." He closed his hand on my upper thigh and pulled it open enough for him to move down on his knees between them.

My pulse jumped into my throat. "What are you doing?" We both knew what he was doing, but I was too weak, too needy, to stop him.

He buried his head between my thighs, pressing his mouth against the lace covering my sex, and let out a groan.

"Dylan." His name fell from my lips like a plea. I squirmed, and it only worked to press more into his mouth as he started sinfully licking the thin fabric covering my swollen clit. I grabbed his thick hair and tugged, my legs widening.

"You're not going to stop me, are you, Brooke," he taunted triumphantly.

I bit my lip to suppress my moan, but I couldn't control my sex from gushing on his tongue that worked around the lace and was lapping against it.

His fingers easily tore through the fabric to give him full access to my bare sensitive flesh trembling against his lips. He inhaled and groaned.

I closed my eyes and took in a sharp breath.

"I should stop," he tormented, giving me a torturously slow swirling of his tongue through my hot folds and up around my clit.

I tightened my grip on his hair. *He'd fucking better not.*

He didn't. He kissed and sucked my pussy with the command of a long-term lover bringing me closer to orgasm with every intimate pass. I pressed and rocked unabashedly against his mouth, taking the pleasure he was willing to give to me. There was no doubt, my body wanted him. I quivered. "I'm close."

He brushed a kiss against my clit and stopped.

My eyes widened and darted frantically over his face. Surely he wouldn't leave me like this?

He gave me a hard look of challenge as he undid his

pants and freed his big, thick cock. He was beautiful in his anger.

I licked my lips and moved my leg over the back of the couch, showing him my shameless answer. I wouldn't deny him. I wouldn't deny the both of us.

He tore open a condom and put it on, then positioned the crown of his cock right at my entrance. "You think about this when you're with your fucking Collin."

He pushed in with one long, powerful thrust until he was sealed all the way inside of me.

I whimpered and gripped his strong shoulders, my body quaking in shock at the sudden fullness. Dylan cursed, his breath coming heavy and fast, letting me know he was just as affected. He grabbed my leg and put it on his shoulder, pushing in his cock even deeper, and we both moaned in ecstasy.

"That's right, Brooke, fucking feel me," he growled out.

I moaned and arched up to him, catching his erotic rhythm as he thrust his hips and moved his cock hard and fast in and out of me. He felt too good to make him go easy on me. *Go on, Keep taking it all out on me.*

He swiveled his hips, angling his cock to stroke my clit with each thrust as he tucked me, enlivening pleasure spots that had me curling my toes at the bliss he awakened within me. My inner walls pulsed and squeezed as I broke apart at the intensity of the orgasm. Dylan soon followed me. His head fell back, and he cursed my name as he climaxed hard inside of me.

I let out a sob as he eased out, my eyes finding his, wondering if I reflected back the blissful contentment that I briefly found in his.

"This is who I am," he said. "I'm a man that will fuck you like a man. I'm not some gentle fucking friend."

He took off his condom and threw it in the wastebasket. Before I could sit up again, he was up on his feet and out the door without a backward glance.

I wiped away the tears that stung my eyes and hit the couch cushion. Damn it. Why couldn't I just enjoy him?

The only answer I had was the pain that clutched my chest at watching him leave. I was too far gone already.

CHAPTER
TWELVE

Dylan

I put on a fake smile for the cameras as they followed me to my car from Brooke's flat. Fuck, did that go wrong. What the hell was I doing? I never should have gone over and I wouldn't have if she didn't look miserable after she left mine. I get there to assure her about the sex, just to have her throw me over for some bloke named Collin. Me. I have never been thrown over in my life. Even after I got her to confess she won't get off with him, she'd rather be unsatisfied with that muppet than be with me. I'd have thought she was a cock tease, the way she let me finger her pussy and got me hard. But the second I said something she didn't like, she shoved me aside for a wanker. Bullocks. She wanted me and I fucking proved it. I fucking owned her.

She looked at me like she didn't want me to go. Hell, I didn't want to go. My cock was already begging me to go back and take her again, but she needed to stew with her stupid decision. She was scared. All because I said I want to care for her.

Hell, I weirded myself out too—saying I wanted to take care of her—but 'care' could mean a lot of things, like I cared enough to make her come. She was the one who went serious. She could have hidden her feelings, but I was coming to learn that wasn't her way.

Taking care was never in my pillow-talk vocabulary. I never said shite like that, let alone to a woman I just met. It probably came from all that sharing we did about family. She looked so sad when she talked about her father. How he would leave her out to struggle when he could help her.

Brooke was independent and strong. But she was like a little lost girl, seeking his approval. Life was hard enough. You helped those you cared about. She cared about them.

She needed someone to care and make her feel good. I knew I could make her feel good. But I wanted to make her a mate, and I tried to make her off-limits by keeping my cool. That was until she dropped those shorts and I got to see her pussy. She was adorably embarrassed. But I could see her swollen clit, and I knew she was wet. I had to taste her. And from that one taste, I couldn't get enough. The way she trembled under my hands when she came… She was so responsive. Genuine. There was nothing fake about her and that made it even better. She had the head of my cock straining in my shorts to get inside of her.

She was good at sucking my cock too, and I was about ready to push her down and fuck her, but then Salvatore and Nicola had shown up. A call about the charity was good enough. I'd have participated. I didn't agree to drop-ins. I argued the pair of them out when Brooke left. No one shows up at my flat uninvited. No one decides who I fuck. If I wanted to fuck Nicola, I'd have already made that happen on my own. I didn't want her.

I fucking wanted Brooke. One time wasn't enough for me, but she chose to run. I said "care" to her twice, and I didn't bolt. She was so sure I would. The thing was, I couldn't promise I wouldn't. There were no promises. We had just met. We'd have to see how things went. She was looking for me to assure her she wouldn't get hurt. I couldn't do that. But I could do right by her in bed. I'd spoil her. She couldn't slow down and enjoy herself? Women.

I chewed my lip. Her loss. Taking out my phone, I called Knox. He was always out and a drink would do me. "Which bar are you in?"

"Hello. How are you doing?" Knox joked. "You going out? I thought you were over at country girl's tonight, riding that sexy ass of hers. Shit, I fucking almost nutted when she put her leg—"

"Shut it. Which bar?" I griped.

"Fuel. VIP," he said. I told my driver.

It took twenty minutes in weekend traffic to get there. However, the second I did, I walked straight on past the bouncers and was escorted over to the VIP section of the nightclub. It was good to be known and not have to wait. But once I arrived, I realized it was a mistake. That arse-hole Tyler was there, finger-fucking a blonde in the corner while another woman had her hands down his pants on his cock. He didn't care where he fucked or what they might record. Knox wasn't any better. He was sucking jello shots off a pair of big tits. "Come take a shot?" he called out.

They were stupid, and I was stupid for showing up here. I turned right around and walked back out.

"I didn't invite him, he showed up," Knox said, catching up to me.

I kept on walking. "I came here to drink."

"Okay, we'll go to another room and drink." I followed him over to the bar in another room and he ordered a Jägermeister and a beer. I half listened as he started talking about everything and nothing. A couple of women came over to where we were and giggled at him, like everything he said was funny, annoying the fuck out of me. Brooke wouldn't say we were funny. She'd call us out. Shite. There she was on my mind again.

I reached for the fresh bottle of beer the bartender placed down and a soft hand covered mine. Glancing back, I found a tall woman with perky, small tits and no bra.

"Sorry, I thought it was mine," she said, grinning.

I moved my hand away and handed it to her. "You can have it."

"You look sad, want to talk about it?" she said.

My eyebrows bunched together. What was this, therapy in the bar? I took my phone out. "I'm alright."

She leaned forward, and I got up and moved away toward the door, ignoring the calls from Knox to return, and I sent for my driver to come get me. I had noticed I had missed a call from my mum and went outside to play it.

"Rocco is well enough to travel and he is on his way. I sent the details for you to get him at the airport. We love you."

I smiled. It was too late to call Manchester. I was about to turn off my phone when I caught a glimpse of a picture of Brooke smiling next to the dog on a subway platform. Her smile brought on that odd feeling again. Shite, I had fucked up us ever being mates. I wanted to fuck her too badly, and I'd done it. Now I still had to work with her. I wouldn't ruin her opportunity or mine.

I was about to press the delete button, but put her photo back in where it was. Nothing wrong with having a look, I supposed. And I did all the way back home.

CHAPTER
THIRTEEN

Brooke

"How are things with Dylan?" My mom asked on our Sunday call.

"Great, Mom," I lied.

I hadn't seen or heard from Dylan since we had sex after our Thursday night fight. Since then, I struggled to get through the rest of the week, including my weekend morning shifts at Colby's and my rehearsal for my debut performance. I had to wonder if he had changed his mind, but Raymond would have told me. Was he seeing Nicola? The thought of him touching her the way he touched me made me crazy with jealousy.

"Tell her we received the money from the last loan I gave her. Has she settled her bank account?" my father shouted in the background, bringing me back to the call.

"Do you want to speak with her?" my mother said, her tone sharp. The line went quiet and my mother audibly sighed. "Your dad said—"

"I heard him, tell him I did," I yelled back. "Thanks."

"I've put the money aside for when she needs to borrow again," he bellowed with sarcasm in his tone.

I hunched my shoulders. "I'm working now. Did you tell Father about my show?"

"Yes. He's so happy and proud of you," she said.

I paused to wait to hear him say as much, but he didn't. "Oh. Okay. Well, I've got to go. Gemma and I are heading out for a celebration breakfast."

"Alright. You coming to Seattle soon?" she asked.

"Maybe," I mumbled. The New York City Football Club had a game there. I wasn't sure if I was still going, but I hadn't heard otherwise, yet.

"Good, I miss you, Brooke."

"I miss you too." I choked and hung up.

After a quick shower, I changed into a pair of skinny jeans and a scoop-neck top and my fancy sneakers. They turned out to be quite comfy. Once I was ready, I found Gemma standing by the door waiting for me.

"Hello, Pierbrooke!" she teased.

I rolled my eyes. "Did you make that up?"

"Nope. It's online." She showed me on her phone as we walked down the street to our favorite local restaurant. The paparazzi were out in numbers this morning.

I secured my dark glasses firmly in place and kept a tight smile as the photographers snapped our photos at the entrance. "Have you seen Dylan?"

"I bet you'd know if I had," I joked and laughed.

"Did you two have a fight? Is that why he was out at the bar with another woman?"

My stomach muscles twisted, but I managed to keep my smile inside the doors. The hostess, whom we had seen many times, stepped forward and personally escorted us to a private booth in back. I didn't have time to marvel at the change in treatment. I had my phone out and pressing hard on the keys as I typed a message to Dylan.

Brooke. S: What the hell are you doing out at a bar with some bimbo!

I got an immediate response.

Dylan M. Pierce: Cool your jets. I stopped at a bar for a drink a few nights ago. The press has hearsay, no photo.

Brooke. S: Oh. But maybe we should see each other to clear any rumors?

Dylan M. Pierce: Alright. I'm at Nicola's. Where are you?

I grimaced, but I gave him the address.

Dylan M. Pierce: You'll have to come out. Rocco is with me. I'll stop by before heading back up town.

I perked up. Doggie. I then deflated. Dylan said his dog was personal, but he brings him around Nicola. Were they together now?

Brooke. S: Thanks.

He didn't respond. I was about to put my phone away but found a new message from Collin.

CollsB495: Did you break up with Dylan Pierce? I heard about Rent. Congrats. I'm at the theater down the street dancing. If you want to hang out.

I smirked. Apparently Collin read the tabloids too. Hang out was our code for "sex." I wrote back.

Brooke.S.: No. Dylan and I are still together. Thank you about Rent. I'm excited about the show.

"What?" Gemma asked, taking a sip of the mimosas our waitress delivered for us I told her about his message.

"You're popular now," she said. "Collin's trying to bang Dylan's girlfriend. That would make a great story. I doubt Dylan would be the sharing kind, so be careful."

I bit my lip. Yeah. It would. That scratched Collin off my list.

"Anyway, let's toast our steps on the road to success," she said.

I lifted my mimosa and drained the glass.

She laughed. "I have news for the both of us. *Les Misérables* has an open call for a national tour! We must audition."

My pulse sped up. "When is it?"

"In a couple of weeks," she replied enthusiastically. "Imagine the two of us on tour. It would be national exposure. I have a great chance too, and if I do, we'll sublet our place for the six months."

"If both of us get it," I said.

"Who's not going to want Dylan Pierce's girlfriend on tour?" It was a tease, but my stomach churned. Was that what I would end up being at the end of this?

"Stop. You're a great talent, Brooke," she recovered. "You are good enough for the lead."

"And so are you," I said, and we ate our breakfast burritos. "What about the apartment?"

"We'll sublet it. Our landlord Yuri loves us. He'd let us, and if not, we will make enough money on the tour to get a better place," she said.

I soaked in her optimism, though I was conflicted. A national tour would mean national exposure, but it would also mean ending what I had with Dylan. It wasn't going to last forever, but the thought of never seeing him again bothered me. No matter how things went, he had affected me and touched me in ways like no other.

We finished up our breakfast and were on our second mimosas when the hostess came over to our table with a toothy grin. "Mr. Pierce would like for you to come to the door. He took care of your bill."

My pulse sped up at seeing him again as we left our seats. We went out the front and found Dylan standing there with Knox. He was dressed in a button-down shirt and denim. His man-bun was high on his head with most of his face covered by a pair of designer sunglasses. He still looked delectable. He was holding Rocco, his husky dog, on a leash, who perked up the second I approached. I immediately went down on the ground to roust and pet him. "Hello, Rocco. Who's a good boy...who's a good boy."

"I am," Dylan deadpanned.

Gemma and Knox fell into fits of laughter.

"Shouldn't you be kissing me before Rocco?" Dylan said. His tone was light, but when I looked over at him he hadn't removed his sunglasses. A few flashes from cameras let me know the paparazzi were out and at a close distance.

I stood, and he gave me a kiss on my lips and I pressed in, moving my hands around his neck. I missed him.

He hugged me back, but eased me gently out of his arms.

"I'm Knox," I heard Knox say to Gemma behind us.

"Yeah, I know," she said and giggled.

"You a fan?" he mused.

"Of Arsenal," she said, and he groaned. They laughed.

"You guys want to come up?" Gemma asked them. "We have some time before we go to work."

Knox grinned at her. "Yeah. We could hang out for an hour, but that won't be enough time." He left for what hanging in the air that thickened between them.

I looked at Gemma and rolled my eyes. He sure moved fast.

She lifted her brows. So did she.

"No. We have things to do," Dylan said, but he didn't elaborate.

"Where is Rocco going?" I asked as he nudged my leg to pet him. "If you need a doggie sitter for the afternoon..."

"No, thanks," he said. "Nicola found a sitter for him."

I rubbed Rocco's head. "I thought Rocco was personal,

141

but I suppose Nicola and you are personal now."

"Jealous?" he asked.

I focused on Rocco who was now licking my chin. "What do you think?"

"If I was sure, I wouldn't ask." He cleared his throat. "Rocco was with Knox and I at a children's hospital charity that will be a part of the runway show. Nothing is going on with me and Nicola. We are strictly professional," he said. "Not that I have to explain myself," he added under his breath.

I exhaled and stood up. "That's great, not about you not being with Nicola—I don't want you with her. I think the hospital work is great."

How many ways can I say "great?" I inwardly admonished myself.

Dylan pulled me into his arms, stealing my breath. His mouth was close to my ear. "That's the last answer you get from me. You made your choice about us. Right?"

I inhaled. "Yeah. You did too. When you walked out after you had me."

He grabbed my waist and pulled me hard against his body, forcing me to laugh it off as Gemma and Knox laughed behind us. He let me go long enough to place his sunglasses on his head. His pale blue eyes were hot and penetrating as they bore into mine. "You know I fucking didn't want to leave you. We were both angry." He brushed his lips against mine. "Why don't you stop fighting me and let me have you?"

I bit the inside of my cheek as the seconds that felt like minutes passed in his arms. My body was heating up at the idea of letting him have me. He'd have me for how long? Long enough for me to get attached and for him to cast me aside for someone else. He was right, I was scared. Mostly of how he made me feel already when I was with him. He could have me in pretend, but I wasn't ready to risk my heart.

He let me go and took my hand and we all walked the few blocks back to our house. Gemma and Knox were chatting away while Dylan and I remained silent, though smiling. When we got there, his car was waiting.

"Good luck with your show." I blinked up at him.

"Thanks," he said and hugged me again, and I clung to him again and he let me hold on until I let go of him. His Adam's apple bobbed up and down. "Good luck with your show. We can do a few more of these meetings during the week."

"You can still call me too, if you want. I'd like to know how you and Rocco are doing," I said hopefully.

He gave me a chaste kiss but didn't answer.

Rocco whined, and I bent down and hugged him. Turning away, I waved to Knox and rushed into my apartment.

And that was pretty much how our meetings went over the next week: Dylan being cold but polite, and me trying to engage in conversation with him. The only one giving me any real attention was Rocco, who loved me from the start.

I had Dylan, but didn't. Sure, he kissed, hugged, and smiled like he was mine, but instantly left the second our publicity show was done.

I had to play up my part too. I drank the iced coffee at a café. I took his rides home from my rehearsals. I even watched a team practice from the sidelines. Everything captured for all public purposes, and it was working. Overnight we had become a new budding couple that social media was curious about. Raymond informed me his phone had been buzzing non-stop to get the two of us together for promotions. We could be booked through the next three months past our initial six-week agreement. If. That was the hard part. And I was happy. Sort of.

The long hours of rehearsing drained most of my energy and I was more than happy to drop into bed at the end of the day. Still, I found I couldn't stop thinking of Dylan. The more I thought about him, the less of a reason I had not to have sex with him. I had all the pros and cons laid out too.

Pros

Drop dead gorgeous

Mouthwatering body I haven't had a chance to touch all of yet

Orgasm-overachiever

Great angry fucking

Thoughtful, funny, and sweet

Easy to talk to though he has a dirty mouth

He's direct, interested, caring

Cons

Cocky—his ego needs its own zip code

Sort of my boss

Yikes! No way.

Our secret relationship going bad and messing up our public one

Falling in love and getting too attached to him

Even so, I wanted Dylan as he really was, not the one I worked with. I wanted the real him. I wanted to be with him, but I didn't know how to tell him. After all, he said he didn't go back. Unfortunately, I had passed up my chance.

The night of the performance finally came, and I was backstage changing into my 1990's costume of a crop top, orange sweater and low hanging cords. My red hair was twisted up in two pony-tail twists. I looked down at the cast list and a thrill went through me. My name was listed as part of the ensemble of a Broadway show. A big step toward my acting dreams.

I loved the musical *Rent*. Never had the message of the show sunk in as much as it had while I'd been working on it. To me it was about loving and embracing the love and the life you have now and appreciating the friends who help build that life. I only wished I had someone special to spend tonight with. I wish I had Dylan.

"Brooke," one of the cast members called for the shows warm-up. We all started to sing "La Vie Bohème." When we were done, we all moved to the back and waited to take our places for the performance.

A stagehand came up to me with a card and a basket of pink M&M's.

"This was delivered to the side door."

My brows disappeared under my bangs as I thanked him and opened the card. It had a car service pass, and a note.

> **The candy reminded me of you and your silly pink trainers.**
> **They don't melt as good in my mouth or taste as delicious.**
> **The real gift is in the envelope. No more night rides on the subway back to your dodgy apartment. Break a leg tonight.**
> **Dylan**

A flutter went through my chest. He didn't do hearts and flowers but he did candy, car service and dirty notes. Honestly, I didn't care about the car service. I wanted Dylan Pierce. And though I was still scared of what this could do now that things were going well, I wasn't frightened enough not to be with him.

I sent a text message that read:

Brooke. S: I want you as you are, Dylan Pierce. I miss you. I'm ready. You ask and I'll come.

"Ten minutes, everyone."

I went to my locker and put my stuff away before joining the cast on stage for the show opener, "Seasons of Love." Then I went to take my place along the aisle for the performance of *Rent*. I did a cartwheel and flip down the aisle, ending in the splits to my mark in front of the audience.

It was exhilarating and thrilling how fast the show passed by. Before I knew it, we were doing the final song, "Finale B" and the film of the cast started rolling on stage. I sang out with all my heart. My acting career was still alive and thriving. I was performing live on Broadway!

After the standing ovation and curtain calls, I hugged the cast and went over to my locker to change. I put on my skirt and top, then took out my phone, debating calling my mom. On my way out the door, however, I was stopped by the crowd on the stage. I went to see who was there and my heart stopped. Dylan was in the middle, surrounded by cast members.

He projected an energy that was powerful, and undeniably attracted all those around him. He must have come straight from the fashion show. He looked like a dark fallen angel with his wings clipped. The front of his spandex shirt was sheer and showed off every ripple of definition of his magnificent muscular frame. The pants he had on were looser than the top and hung low, right on the V at his hips. His hair was braided back from his sculpted face, which had shimmer makeup highlighting his pale blue eyes, making them glimmer. He looked achingly beautiful.

Once he spotted me, his compelling gaze was on me, and in it I found his call.

I went without hesitation over to him and into his arms where he lifted me up into a tight hug. "I missed the beginning, but what I did get to see, you were amazing."

I tightened my grip around his neck and he sealed his lips against mine. I could hear the shutters flashing around us. This time I kept my leg down while we held on to each other. When he placed me back on my feet, he cupped my face and kissed me tenderly on my lips. However, before he let me go, he said, "This is for the press. You're going to make up for making me jacking off all week."

I grinned as a thrill of anticipation shot through my body. That was Dylan. I could only nod. I wanted him as much as he wanted me.

He placed his hand in the middle of my back and moved us toward the exit.

"Brooke?" I turned to find Collin standing there. He had on a dress shirt and jeans. He had grown a beard since the last time I saw him. His hair was back in a ponytail.

"Collin," I announced, answering Dylan's pointed stare. He tensed next to me.

Goosebumps broke across my skin as his hand moved around me, stopping low on my bare stomach.

"You were amazing," he said.

I went to move, but Dylan tightened his hold on my waist. I sighed and lifted my hand and outstretched it formally.

Collin glanced down at my hand and shook it.

"Dylan Pierce! Big fan," Collin said enthusiastically. "Would you sign my program?"

"Sure," Dylan said and scrawled his signature and handed it back, keeping me right next to him. "We have to go."

"Alright…thanks for coming," I said to Collin over my shoulder.

Dylan steered us into his car, avoiding the press, and we took off.

"What was that all about?" I asked.

"You're with me. He needed to know," he said with annoyance in his tone.

I licked my lips. "What about Nicola?"

"What about her?" he asked, his tone abrupt. "She's my lawyer. End of. I've already told you this."

I narrowed my gaze. "And that's how it will have to be with all women, Dylan, as long as we are…friends with benefits. I don't share. This isn't about pressuring you into a relationship, but it has to work for the both of us. I don't share."

"I don't either," he said, his tone sharp. "That's the last time Collin comes around you."

I rolled my neck. "I didn't know Collin was coming, and I told him I was with you."

He scoffed. "Now he's heard from the both of us. I can't tell Nicola about us, but I've been clear I won't be with her. As for Collin—"

I shook my head. "You're being silly. I don't want Collin. I want… I mean, I'm here with you."

He captured my chin. "No, you want me." He ran his thumb over my bottom lip. "Say it."

I parted my lips and ran my tongue along the tip. He needed to hear it. "I want you, Dylan," I said.

He pushed his thumb into my mouth and I sucked on it. "Fuck. I want you to suck the head of my dick just like that."

I moaned as he trailed his thumb down my chin and to the top of my boobs, down to trace the outline of my taut nipples.

"I should strip you naked right now," he said and lightly bit down on the tip.

I took in a ragged breath as I arched my back up to him. "We can't here, or can we?"

"No, but we can where I'm taking you," he said, pushing my shirt up impatiently and cupping one of my breasts. "We'll pick you up in the back of your building in an hour," he said. "Bring your clothes for Toronto."

I closed my hand around his. "Where are we going?"

"We are going to Toronto like I said, but for tonight... off the grid," he said. "Where I can do whatever I want with you."

A shiver of anticipation went through me. "Okay."

He chuckled. "Okay? No protesting."

I shook my head "I want that too, but what about the flight to Toronto?"

"We'll make it," he said. His hands moved down to rub my ass. "Don't bother with lingerie unless you don't want to keep them."

I moved back into the seat to look at him. My eyes darted around his face. "Did you keep my...panties from Thursday?" I asked.

"Yes," he said casually. "I jerked off on them. You want them back?"

I swatted him and he grabbed my wrist and laughed. Our gazes connected and my heartbeat skipped. "I missed you."

"Me too," he said and pulled me closer to him. "I can't wait to get inside of you." He kissed down my neck and up to my ear.

I moaned and squirmed next to him. "I need you inside me now."

"I will fuck you right here," he teased.

"Go on and do it," I goaded, and rubbed the top of his thigh. He let me do it until I rubbed over the bulge in his pants.

"Behave," he said and removed my hand. "We still have our public image. I can't have you looking fucked coming out of this car."

I batted my long eyelashes. "I could act innocent."

His lips parted as he trailed his hand down the side of my face. "I'm sure you could, but we will wait until we're alone. I appreciate how frustrated you are." He kissed the side of my face. "The second I have you alone, you're all mine and I will…"

He didn't finish.

A pang went through my chest at my making him change what was in his heart for me.

"If you want to care, I'm here to accept," I whispered.

I felt his chest expand as he tucked me against him, but he didn't answer.

I snuggled in. He didn't have to. I had Dylan Pierce for real, and I was content.

CHAPTER
FOURTEEN

I had enough time to take a shower, pack, and answer my well-wishing messages from my mother, Raymond, and friends, before putting on a shirt and skirt (no undies) to meet Dylan at the back of my building. He was already there when I arrived, sitting behind the driver's seat of a Mercedes SUV with the interior lights on. He was no longer dressed in that fancy fashion show apparel, but a pair of jeans and a loose fitting gray shirt. His hair was tied up in a knot and back from his face, his skin pulled taut over the elegant ridges of his cheekbones as he concentrated on the phone he held in his hand. He was insanely hot.

I tapped on the glass on the passenger's seat window and he immediately put his phone away and was out of the car to greet me. A bark from Rocco let me know he had come along for our getaway.

My hand trembled a little as I handed over my bag to him.

"You nervous?" He put it down on the ground and

cupped my face.

"A little," I admitted.

He brushed his lips against my forehead. "You should be," he said darkly.

I let out a giggle, and he pulled me into a hug and I wrapped my arms around him and inhaled. He smelled freshly showered.

"We already had sex, so what has you nervous?" he asked.

"I don't know," I lied.

His allure and tenacity was part of it, though not all. What I feared the most was my brain thinking his kindness meant he was really into me, but I couldn't bring myself to say it.

He sighed. "I think you do, but you will be fine, I promise." He kissed me tenderly on the lips. "Now get in before Rocco tries to break his cage to get to us."

On cue, Rocco let out a happy bark and we both laughed. He opened the back door, and I climbed on the seat to try to pet Rocco through his carrier.

"I didn't know you were bringing him," I said cheerfully.

"I brought him so no one will know I'm not around. Settle down," Dylan ordered. Rocco let out a whine before lying back on his bed.

"How is he doing?" I asked.

"He's knackered. The dog-walker took him out for a two-hour walk. He should sleep well tonight while we're up together."

He helped me up into my seat as a thrill worked through me at his words. We were going to spend the night and part of the day alone together. I wondered just what he would do with me. It took me a few seconds to notice he hadn't moved from my side of the door and when I did he commanded, "Pull up your skirt."

My chest heaved as I eased the fabric up my legs enough for him to reach under and cup my sex.

A muscle ticked in his jaw. "Fuck. No panties."

I licked my lips. "Well, you're the one who said not to wear them."

"This is mine now. That's how I want you to think of it. I'll touch, taste, and fuck it anytime I want to." His voice sounded like gravel.

I moaned and grew wetter under his hand as he massaged my sensitive flesh, teasing my clit.

"Mm…you like that," he said with a groan. "You need me inside you right now, Brooke? Show me."

"Yes, I do," I rasped and gulped as he pushed two fingers inside me.

I closed my eyes and rocked my hips, moving as he pumped me with them.

"Christ, you're bad when you're horny," he mused, and pulled his fingers out and placed them in his mouth and sucked. I squirmed in my seat as I watched his sensual act. He then kissed me passionately, giving me a taste of myself.

"See how sweet you are?" he purred.

My face warmed.

"You blushing down to your pussy again for me?" He lifted my skirt higher.

I whimpered and grabbed my skirt. "Please stop teasing me and drive or are we doing it here?"

His face softened in the interior lights. "Not this time. I want you stretched out under me."

My heart skipped a beat. "I want that too," I whispered. "How far?"

"It'll be a short drive to Long Island." he gave me a peck before closing the car door and proceeding to drive us out of the East Village, and New York City.

We drove into Long Island, through a tree-lined suburban neighborhood. I barely saw the driveway by the massive trees surrounding it. Sitting like a beacon in the middle was a modern two-story stone home, the three rows of windows reflected in the headlights.

"This is my getaway place. I got it a while back when I thought about staying in New York City permanently," Dylan said as he pressed the button on the garage and drove us in and parked.

He took my bags and let me get his dog out, and we all crossed through a spacious, white and stone kitchen and over to glass patio doors. He took Rocco off the leash and he skidded down the wooden stairs off the polished deck, doing four laps around the covered pool before he started his lazy wander around the fenced in property.

My heart warmed at the joy on his face as we played with his dog a bit before bringing him back inside the house to settle down in what appeared to be his own little doggie room that was complete with an electronic feeder and a huge doggie bed with his name on it.

"Chic," I teased.

"He's my buddy," he said softly and patted his fur.

I bent down and touched his shoulders and pressed a kiss to his neck. Dylan turned and deepened the kiss. We both wanted more and, as was Dylan's way, he went with the moment. He helped me to stand and led me up a flight of carpeted stairs to a large master bedroom with a king-sized bed, boasting white decorative bedding, then into a large gray and white tiled bath with an oval tub and walk-in shower.

"You can clean up in here and I'll use the one in the guest room. Don't bother with clothes," he said and opened the top drawer in the built-in cabinet that was full of toiletries.

"You have many visitors?" The words were out of my mouth before I could stop them.

"I've had Knox and some of the other players down," he answered.

I hid my face and took a fresh toothbrush.

"No. I don't bring women down here, but... I suppose you're the exception," he said and smirked. "Your character has a real problem with passive-aggressive jealousy."

I swiped his arm. "And your character is very direct in his jealousy."

"Sure the hell am," he said and swatted my buttocks hard with his hand. "Don't forget it."

"Ouch, fine. I'm not usually the jealous type, but..." My voice trailed off.

"But with me you are," he finished for me and rubbed soothingly over my ass cheeks before walking out, not waiting for the rest of my answer. I smiled. He didn't need one.

I went about stripping and cleaning up alone before padding across the cool tile floor to the bedroom. When I returned, the side lamps were on and Dylan was lying down with the sheets stretched out, naked and propped up on his elbow facing me. Waves of heat pooled between my thighs as my eyes roved over his tempting, attractive, male physique. His gaze held just as much desire as he looked over my body.

"Come here," he directed and ran his hand over the space next to him on the bed where he wanted me.

I timidly crossed to the bed and lay on my back, close to him.

He moved up on his knees and took my hand and kissed the back of them before moving them with gentle authority up to the headboard. "Keep your hands up here while I explore what is mine now."

I squinted at him and sighed. "I let that comment slide by in the car, but please don't say what you don't mean. Let's just enjoy ourselves?"

"Damn it, Brooke. I never say what I don't mean… your body belongs to me now."

I gave a weak smile. "I know you say that to turn us on, but I'm warning you to be careful with me. I like you—"

"And I like you too," he cut me off. "That goes both ways. I don't know what this is…"

"Neither do I, but I just ask you to try." I couldn't bring myself to say the rest, but he understood. I was afraid of getting hurt.

He gazed into my eyes. "We could hurt each other, but what I know is that I want you."

I smiled up at him. "I want you too, Dylan."

The delight on his face warmed my insides. His hands and mouth moved over me, my body arched and melted into his touch as his hands explored the curves of my back, waist and hips. His hands sought out pleasure points on my thighs, the backs of my knees, and my lower back. When he reached them, he paused and whispered his claim over each part of my body, sealing each claim with his kiss.

He moved back up to my mouth and kissed me. "You are so beautiful, Brooke."

My throat felt suspiciously tight, and I closed my eyes and wrapped my arms and legs around him, pulling him down on top of me in a hug.

"I've got you." He rocked his cock against my soaked pussy lips, both of us moaning at the sensual friction.

"That was gentle. Why did you do that?" I whispered.

"Because you're precious and I want to enjoy what you gave me. Let me have some more," he said in a low rumble. I felt myself gush between my thighs and he ground against me again, this time the head of his cock slipping inside.

"Mmm…that for me?" he mused. "I'll taste you first. You want that, Brooke?"

"Yes," I whispered against his lips. I released my hold, and he pulled my hands back up to the headboard.

My breath came faster as he kissed down to my breasts, cupping and kneading them with his hands.

"These are perfect," he groaned and rubbed over

the surface from his forehead down to his mouth where he captured my nipple between his lips. His tongue caressed my swollen nipples with tantalizing possessiveness. The gentle massage of his mouth sent currents of desire through me as he rolled and pinched my nipples.

My fingers gripped the wood tighter, my back arching up in offering. "Yes," I hissed.

Moving on down to my stomach, his tongue teased my belly button before he pressed it over my clit and through my folds. Goosebumps raced over my skin. My inner walls clenched with every lash of his tongue, and I writhed as he rocketed me straight up to my climax.

"Dylan," I moaned.

"I got you," he groaned and tongued me more fiercely until I yelled out his name as my orgasm exploded through me. Dylan swiftly moved up my body. His eyes were dark with lust, his jaw tense. "Fuck, Brooke. The way you come on my tongue drives me crazy. I need to be inside you right now. I can't wait any longer."

Pushing my legs farther apart with his knee, Dylan covered me with his hot, hard body and with one wicked thrust, he sheathed himself deep inside me.

"Damn, *my* pussy feels so fucking good," he cried out reverently.

I moaned, my fingers aching as I held on to the headboard. *Yes. All of me, yours.*

He started to relentlessly pound his thick cock inside me. Passion heated through my blood as pleasure exploded over me.

"Fuck. I don't think I can last. Tight pussy feels too damn good. Come for me, love." I didn't know how I could come when he commanded it, but at that very moment I did, my inner muscles constricting on his big cock. That's when he lost it, slamming faster and harder inside me until he hissed and his whole body shuddered, his hot cum spurting deep inside of me. My pussy still gripped him tight, milking him.

He looked down at me in shock, eyes wild. "I didn't use a condom. I never…"

He started to pull out but I tightened my legs around his hips, gripping the sides of his face. "I'm on the implant, remember? We discussed this, it's okay."

Still looking a little shell-shocked, I took that moment to push him onto his back, straddling him and moved his cock back inside of me. He instinctually grabbed my ass, pulling me down as he pushed himself up, trying to get deeper. He groaned. "Give me a minute. I'm not done with you yet."

I pressed my lips against his chest. "Can I touch you?"

"My cock?" He wiggled his hips, and I felt the beginnings of his cock swelling again inside me.

I lifted my head up and smiled at him. "Not just your cock, Dylan. Can I touch your body? I've wanted to and haven't had a chance."

His lips parted, and his eyelids dropped to half-mast. Was he suddenly shy? I'd never guess. He licked his lips and whispered, "Go on."

Smiling, I pressed a kiss to his lips, then eased him out of me.

I traced my hand over the chiseled features of his face, my lips kissing over his stubbled jaw and down his neck to the steely muscles of his arms and chest. I could feel Dylan's stare as he patiently waited while I lay my own claim on him. And with his quiet acceptance, my hands roamed freer and bolder as I touched the muscular ridges of his chest down to his abs where I kissed the soft trail of hair that led to his beautiful, resting cock. I didn't stop there, though. I kissed and licked over his shaft and down to the soft hair on his sac then down to his muscle-toned thighs. Getting him to turn over, I kissed over the cheeks of his firm buttocks.

Dylan rolled over and reached for my rear. He ran his hand down the crack to the lips of my sex to tease my swollen clit. "I'm ready for more." He was—appearing full and erect already.

"Soon," I whimpered and continued my exploration over his legs and down to touch his feet that had me smiling. They were pretty too.

"God, you're beautiful," I whispered.

Dylan sat up and pulled me into his arms. "You're the beautiful one of us." He kissed me, then turned me over, his hand moving to stroke my clit. "Move up on your knees," he instructed. I moved to follow, and he positioned himself behind me. His hands gripped my buttocks and then lifted me up and entered me from behind. I closed my hands around the sheets and pulled as he flexed his hips to move deeper until our thighs touch. He cursed. I felt my inner muscles squeeze around his cock, and it was my turn to curse.

"Oh, Brooke, that felt so fucking good. I don't think I'll ever get enough of you." He clasped my sides and swiveled his hips, easing in and out of me in short, sharp thrusts.

I matched his rhythm, pushing my hips back for more. "Dylan. Fuck." He felt so good. I was close to the point of no return and I moved my hips faster, setting a different pace.

A hard swat landed across my rear.

I looked back and Dylan had on one of his devilish grins. He cocked an eyebrow. "You want more?"

I giggled. "Go on."

That was all he needed. He timed his swats with every powerful thrust and I bucked back in what became a feverish pace. My body burned and enlivened with every pass until I cried out, "Dylan, I'm coming."

He squeezed my sore ass as he ground his cock in, and I exploded, screaming as I climaxed. He pistoned his hips and called out my name as he came hard inside me. Our breaths came heavier as we collapsed down on the bed to recover. I whimpered at my sore butt as I felt Dylan's lips kissing and gently rubbing over it.

Turning to my side, I whispered, "Hold me, please."

He stretched out and pulled me on top of him. "Anytime you want it," he whispered against my head.

I want you, Dylan Pierce, in any way I can have you.

CHAPTER

FIFTEEN

Dylan

I cocked that right up. What the hell was wrong with me?

I was all about control in the bedroom. Never had I forgotten to use a condom. It was a schoolboy error, not something I ever did, not even when I was young. My coach hammered into my brain that if I did, I might end up with a kid with a woman I didn't want beyond coming inside of her. That would be shitty for all of us. It was responsibility and time I couldn't afford with someone I didn't care about.

My parents had taken in many kids who were left by parents not ready for them. They cared and gave them the best life they could, but there were thousands more that were still left alone. Knowing that had made me extra careful, but I wasn't tonight.

The thing was, I thought about Brooke the whole time I was with her. The sexy noises she made when I touched her, how good she tasted on my tongue, and how she lost control of herself when she came for me. She wasn't doing porn star pouty poses or trying to look sexy. She had no guards up. She was uninhibited, sweet. Sincere. Honest. Genuine. That, I found addicting. Hell, I completely lose myself in her.

Women have tried to please me in bed before, and I always enjoyed the effort, but with Brooke it was different. She touched me like I was something special to her. And, fuck, did that hit me hard in the chest. She wasn't someone I was going to pass back easily. We had the contraception conversation and that should have eased my conscience, but that wasn't all that was bothering me. What got to me was that I didn't think then or even now of *not* being with her. I went even further and marked every inch of her gorgeous body as mine. Her perfect big tits, curvy hips, firm ass, and long legs. It was too early for feelings or ownership. Wasn't it? Shit, she had me second-guessing myself. I was messed up. Hell, she had already charmed Rocco. He had fallen for her.

"Let's shower and get to sleep," I muttered.

She planted a kiss on the center of my chest before lifting up her head. "Okay. You alright?"

I bit into my lip. She was killing me. "Yeah." I was hard again, and she was wiggling on me. I lifted her up and carried her into the bathroom, and she turned the knob on the shower and we stepped inside. The spray ran down over her hair and she threw her head back and laughed. Damn, she was beautiful.

She was still in my arms. I could feel she wasn't just wet from the shower, but I needed to show some control.

Placing her down on the tile, I turned my back to keep myself together and washed over my body. But when I turned around to rinse off, she had her hands between her thighs, soaping up her pussy, making my mouth water and my dick hard again.

"Fuck, Brooke, what are you doing to me?" I groaned.

"What?" she smiled and rinsed off.

I went down on my weakened knees, put her leg on my shoulder and ate her sweet pussy again. I wasn't being gentle about it either. I gave her harsh, punishing strokes of my tongue on her hot clit. My fingers thrust inside her as fast and deep as I wanted to fuck her right there and then. Broke was hot for it. She pressed back into my face, willingly submitting, making my cock ache to get back inside her again.

Oh well. Screw it.

I was on my feet and lifting her up to take her against the tile. My hands squeezed her round ass as I pushed my cock in deep.

"Dylan," she whimpered out my name as she gripped my shoulders. She was probably sore with how hard I kept fucking her. I wasn't small and every glide inside her tight pussy made my dick thicker. She had me fucking lust-drunk. And I wasn't stopping. I needed her this way.

"Take it for me," I gritted out, as I thrusted in hard and fast.

"Yes. For you...yes," she moaned. Her heels dug hard into my ass as I moved in and out of her. Her muscles grabbed ahold of my cock and she shook in my arms, letting me know she was going to come.

I bit down on her neck and sucked her skin as she

screamed out her climax.

I found my own release and yelled out as I came. But I didn't stop. I fucked her until my cock went down and then rubbed it against her folds when I was out of her. I couldn't get enough of her. She didn't stop me either. She wanted the same.

We cleaned up again and dried off. When we returned to the bedroom, my phone went off. I went to pick it up and found it was a text from my mum.

We miss our handsome son. Are you still awake? Can we skype?

Brooke came up to me and asked, "Is everything alright?"

"My parents want to skype from Manchester," I replied.

She tried and failed to hide the excitement on her face.

"If you want to meet them, you can," I said, surprising myself, and ran my hands down her arms.

She shivered. I loved how responsive she was with me.

"Really? They sounded so lovely when you talked about them," she said enthusiastically. "You can introduce me as your friend...but wait,"—she grabbed her messy hair and puckered her brow—"maybe another time."

I kissed her lips. "Now, beautiful." She blushed and didn't that make my dick twitch. I took a deep breath and texted my parents back, informing them she would be on the call too. "They know about you since we are public. It will be short since I have a game later."

"I know it's part of...well, thank you," she stammered. She hugged my waist.

She was fucking adorable. "No. There was no plan to introduce you to them," I told her and kissed her forehead. Her smile went from ear to ear.

I went to my closet and threw her a T-shirt to put on and grabbed a pair of shorts for myself before settling us both in front of the laptop on the desk to make the call.

"You sure about this?" she whispered. Pulling out the chair, I placed her on my lap.

"Yes," I said and kissed her neck. That was how my parents saw us when we appeared on the webcam. They were dressed in casual wear of button-down shirts. My dad appeared to have cut his hair in a crew-cut. My mum's gray hair was bobbed shorter than Brooke's. Her smile went wide, whilst my dad eyed us curiously.

"Hello," my mum sang out. I introduced them, and Brooke launched right away into how much she admired their work as caregivers. My mum went into details of how much she loved children and wanted to have a big family and her lifelong work with children in need.

"Dylan continues our work with his clothing program for children in our town, and a breakfast program for families in need," she said and winked at me.

"It's really not that much," I said and smiled.

"It's amazing. You must be so proud of him," Brooke gushed.

"We are. Maybe he's ready to get married and start his family," my mum teased. "You're the first lady I met not by accident."

Brooke burst with laughter and my mum grinned at her.

"Mum, come on," I moaned. "She already knows that

about me."

"Stop teasing him," my dad said, coming to my aid. "Anything going on with football, son?"

I blew out a breath. "Still playing, for now."

"Not for long. You only signed for a year. You need to keep yourself going. Keep busy for life after sports," my dad said. He was giving me a lecture we had often enough.

I sighed. "I know and something will come soon."

"You can always come back here," my mum said. "You're welcome to come too, Brooke." She meant every word.

Brooke trembled a little in my lap and I gripped her waist. The pressure was on. "Enough, Mum. Don't scare her," I half-joked.

She laughed. "How's Rocco? Did you get him checked out yet?"

"I got an appointment for next week," I replied.

"Does Rocco have an illness?" Brooke asked me.

"No, but he was having trouble eating," I whispered.

She ran her hand over my own.

"You need me to go with you, I will," she said.

I smiled at her and glanced at my parents. They were smiling at the two of us. "We need to go. I have a game later today and I haven't gone to sleep," I said.

My mum's eyes widened and my dad shook his head and smiled at me.

"Good luck and we'd love to hear from the two of you again soon," Mum said.

I rolled my eyes but smiled. "Love you both."

"We love you too." We ended the call.

"They are so kind," Brooke said, her voice thick. I

cuddled her to me. "They are. I'm fortunate...they like you."

"You think so?" She perked up.

"Who wouldn't?" I replied. After turning everything off, I carried her back to bed and stripped us both down before settling her back on my chest to sleep. It felt right having her there.

We had made it in time to drop Rocco at the dog-sitter's and get on the flight to Toronto for the game. It was a 45-minute flight. I only had time to hug Brooke before the cameras and leave with the team.

Unfortunately, none of us were playing our best. We were tied at halftime. Ace, our keeper, was holding, but we were letting him down. Toronto had put every defender they had on me. Knox had been yellow-carded for a simple tackle. I'd have argued the refs were biased to Toronto. And we could usually handle it if it weren't for the way Tyler was playing. He was our only other attacker and needed to step up and do his part, but instead of connecting with our team, he tried again and again to score a goal on his own.

Lance, our midfield captain, already tore him a new arsehole during our time outs, but the barmy bastard never listened. Playing for yourself wasn't how you rose to stardom. It happened when we all played well together. It wasn't a lesson I got when I was younger either, but that wasn't going to save this game. We played on but nothing worked. We were on injury time now and we were going to lose. We had to get it together.

I worked to tune out the crowd that was shouting my name and focused on what play was before me. The ball was kicked by their keeper right in my path. I got around the defenders and lunged forward and connected, passing the ball across field to Knox and took off running.

Stopping near the net, I pointed back at Lance who was on the left corner. I got around defense and got ahead of Tyler who was attempting to volley it for a perfect shot and connected it. The ball spun through the air toward the net and the keeper dove, but only got the tip of his fingers as it hit the back. We won. Knox and Lance rushed over and hugged me.

Tyler came up and brushed my shoulders. "I had it, prick."

"If you had it, you'd have done it, arsehole," I yelled back.

Lance came up between us and moved us off field where we were forced into doing the interviews. I talked about the team and how good Toronto played, but my eyes were searching the stands for Brooke. I wanted her with me.

Moving toward the team exit tunnel, I was bombarded with fans and I stopped to sign some things and take a few of the stolen kisses I couldn't stop from coming. I walked on and took photos with some of the corporate sponsors and their children and was just about inside the locker room before I heard Brooke's voice squeal out from behind me. My pulse sped up, and I held out my arms as she rushed forward to fill them.

"Congratulations on winning," she said. "That was a tense game."

I smoothed her hair back from her face and kissed her. "I'll be right out to take you to the airport. Thank you for coming here for me."

"Salvatore wants to take me." She glanced back, and I saw him staring at us and waved. "It's okay. We will see each other when you get back."

"I'm taking her to the airport," I yelled out, not caring who in the paparazzi heard. She would be cared for by me. I kissed the top of her head, then headed inside to take a shower and listen to Lance and Coach Marron's debriefing. He let us all have it for lack of team effort, but he left it with a bit of encouragement for the rest of the games this week. I stripped down and went into the shower.

"Dinner?" Knox asked.

I gave him a nod. "Seeing Brooke off first."

He grinned. "Pussy must be real good."

"You'll never know," I retorted.

He laughed at me. "You rushing out to her tells me everything, you know. You're screwed."

I grimaced and turned away. Maybe I was.

I went out and found her waiting there for me. She was smiling, but those big beautiful green eyes of hers were unfocused.

"Alright, Brooke?" I asked.

She put on a bright smile. "Yeah."

I frowned. I hated when she lied to me, but I didn't have time to get my answer from her. She needed to get back to New York for her next show performance.

Nicola came sauntering up next to the hired car.

"Hello, Dylan."

I cocked a brow. "I didn't know you were coming to the game. I have Salvatore here."

Her lips parted. "I had the time and, well, we need to go over some of the new contracts today. Salvatore mentioned Raymond had sent you a Pollini script."

My lips perked up, and I looked at Brooke and she acknowledged with enthusiasm over the big news. Pollini was a famous director and his movies were varied, but always winning awards. "Thank you. We can talk about it after I get back."

She grinned. "Alright. I'll meet you in your room." Nicola still had it in her head I'd come back to her, but I wasn't going to.

Brooke folded her arms. Her smile wilted a little. That wasn't going to be the end of it, but I could fix what I could now. "I'm going out with Knox. You can leave the script with Salvatore and I'll see you later if we need to discuss it."

"Oh, we will," she said, smiling at Brooke.

I glared at Nicola before we got in the car and took off. The windows were blacked out, and I quickly put a call in to the driver to park near the private flights. He was from a private company and he was good with celebrities. He knew how to keep his mouth shut. I had gotten her a private flight back, away from the press, as a surprise. It was for selfish reasons too because I wasn't going to let her go off for a few days without having sex with her again. It was then I noticed she was wearing jeans. "Why do you still have those on?" I mused.

"Because we need a sex break," she teased. At least I

hoped that was a tease.

I pulled up her shirt and licked a nipple through her bra. "Why?"

She moaned and ran her hand over my hair. She didn't deny me. "Only for a few days. You'll be back soon. So tell me about the script? Nicola had mentioned it to me during the game."

I lifted my eyebrows. "It was the first time I'd heard about it. We can take a look together if you'd like."

I kissed down to the top of her jeans.

"Good. If you need someone to do lines with…" she offered.

I lifted my head and grinned. "Yeah. I'd like that."

"I want you happy, Dylan. I want you to succeed. Always believe that."

"Why wouldn't I know that?" I asked. "Did Nicola say something to you?"

She lifted a shoulder and lowered her eyelids "Nothing I didn't know."

I cupped the side of her face. "Tell me, now."

She licked her lips. "She said you were together for three months. One minute you guys were together, the next you were on a plane to New York City, with no warning that you were moving there permanently, without her. I believe her little speech was to basically prepare me…"

"Prepare yourself for when I leave you? I haven't even been with you enough for her to give you that stupid warning," I cursed. "I'll have a talk with her, but because things didn't work with her doesn't mean it's the case with you."

"But we're just having fun." She winked at me, then

averted her eyes. She didn't believe that. I didn't either. I put my arm around her and kissed her lips and up to her ear. "Let's just see what works for us."

She leaned in to me. "I want that," she whispered.

"Are you too sore from last night?" I asked, running my hand over her ass. My need for her crowded the space.

"No, just go easy on me," she said and kissed me.

"I will, now open your jeans," I instructed.

She pulled them down enough for me to work my hand inside her knickers and feel her pussy. She was soaking wet.

I grunted. "Fuck. I need inside you, now."

"I need you too, Dylan," she rasped. She pulled her jeans the rest of the way off and I got my dick out for her to climb on. Damn, she felt too good.

Pushing up her top and bra, I sucked on her tits as she rode me. I would have kept it going for a while, but we didn't have much time. Reaching between us, I played with her clit until she shuddered, then grabbed her ass and lifted her to pick up the pace. I loved how it felt fucking her without the condom. I could feel her pussy rippling around me.

"Dylan," she cried out as I lightly pinched her clit. Her pussy practically sucked on my cock as she came. It had me coming right after her.

After we calmed down, I kissed her hard on the lips.

I felt her smile against my neck. "I'm going to miss you, Dylan. Even for a few days—and not because of the sex."

I grinned. "I'm going to miss you too." I kissed her hard on the mouth and when we cleaned up and our clothing was fixed, I helped her get out. She was surprised to see the private plane.

"Dylan, no," she protested.

"Too late, Brooke. This was from a friend of mine. It's good." She still looked worried. I clasped the sides of her face. "I will take care of you in any way I want to. It makes me feel good knowing you'll have a nice flight back."

Her eyes watered. "I don't want you doing this for me. I can take a commercial flight...but thank you." She hugged me.

My chest tightened at her gratitude. She was special.

She tugged on my hair and kissed me. I broke the kiss. The flight had to leave on time. I gave her another quick hug she wanted before leaving my arms for the plane. She stopped in the doorway and blew me back a kiss and I sucked in air. I didn't want her to go. Hell, I even waved before getting back in the car.

Damn. I had to admit it now. Brooke got me.

CHAPTER
SIXTEEN

Brooke

I walked inside my apartment and fell down on my bed. Between rehearsal, performing, and behind-the-scenes work, I kept busy though I counted down the days until Dylan's return to New York City at the end of the week. Since our time alone together, he hadn't left me completely on my own. He called in the early morning and we shared updates on the game and my performance. He also made it a habit of calling in the middle of the night to share every dirty thing he wanted to do to me when he returned. No matter how hard I tried, I was becoming attached to Dylan and Rocco. What was I going to do when he moved on without me?

My doorbell rang and I went to the door and signed for a large envelope before I opened it. *Obsession* by Andre Pollini, with a note:

Guard this with your life. I get caught sharing this script and it's over. I'd love to know what you think about it. I'll call you later. Rest up for tomorrow night.
Dylan

I sent a text.

Brooke.S.: Thanks for the package. So excited. I can't wait to see you. I miss you.

My pulse raced as I went to erase the "miss you" part, but it was already sent. Then again, he said he missed me back at the airport. My conversation with Nicola during the game had been making me second-guess myself. She had pretended not to suspect a thing, but she was direct in what would happen with Dylan.

"Brooke?"

Nicola took the empty seat next to me.

"I know you say you're not with Dylan, but I can see the way he behaves with you, it will only be a matter of time."

"It won't. We're friends," I said and stared out at the field, but she continued to speak to me.

"Three months I was his world, then he received the job with the New York Football Club, and he immediately broke up with me."

I glanced at her. "Is that why you came to New York?"

"No. I've always lived between New York and England. I was hired to help him. He often mixes business with pleasure," she said.

I shrugged and clapped along with the crowd.

She touched my arm to get my attention again. "You seem like a nice girl, I'm not trying to upset you, but just to let you know what I wished someone would have told me. L.A. is his target. He just got a Pollini script."

My pulse sped up. "That's great! He must be so excited."

"He will be and he will succeed, he always does. However, when it happens for him, he'll leave you behind. He's not going to do anything but date you. No matter how much you love him, he will never love you back. Be smart and prepare yourself for your next step without him."

A pang went through my chest and I focused out on the field. She hadn't said anything I hadn't thought myself. I peered at her through my lashes. "If we were together, I'd know he wasn't serious about me, and I'm fine."

Her smile broadened. "Good…you know I could introduce you to the Leighton brothers. If you'd like to continue dating celebrities."

I chewed my bottom lip. "Thank you for the offer, but I can get my own dates."

"Alright. Enjoy the game," she said and sauntered away.

A few hours later I closed the Pollini script and fell back on my bed. It had everything a Pollini script was known for: originality, passion, drama. More so the male lead, Gavin, encompassed all the qualities of the man I had come to know. He was, by description, striking in features, but he was also dominant, determined, confident and ardent. This role could be his ticket to superstardom and I had no doubt that he would get it. Their next away game was against the LA Galaxy. Would he be meeting with them there? My eyes teared up, and I took a deep breath. I was losing him sooner than I thought. There I was again. We were dating. We weren't officially a couple. He was doing what he needed to do with his career, and I needed to focus on doing what I needed to do with mine.

Rising up from the bed, I went into the bathroom and splashed cold water on my face and then put in a call to Raymond. Q Studios had scheduled me for their shoot, and I needed his pep to get me there. His phone rang out and went to voicemail. By the time I finished leaving the message, he called back.

"Hey, Brooke. I remembered your appointment for Q Studios. Good luck tomorrow."

I bit my lip. "Thanks. Uhm…anything else in the pipeline that I could audition for?"

"Not yet, but I do have some interest," he replied. "How is *Rent* going?"

I sat down on the couch. "Great. Thanks."

"Maybe they'll make you a permanent part of the cast. That would be a good start," he said brightly. He was giving his usual pep talks, but today it wasn't working.

"Yeah, it would be," I said.

"Alright, I'll talk to you later. Good luck." Before he hung up, I blurted, "I'm going for *Les Misérables* The open auditions are in a couple of days."

"The touring company auditions? I have Gemma down for that call. You do realize that if you are cast it'll be for six-months. That would mean you wouldn't be Dylan's girlfriend anymore if you get it. Did you discuss this with him?"

I let my hair fall in my face. "No, but we all must do what works best for us," I said. My voice graveled.

He blew out into the phone. "I can't stand in your way from trying out, of course, but try to stay positive. With the new cards, things could come in any day. It's all about timing. Your time will come."

"Yeah, I'll think on it." My call-waiting went off, and we ended the call. I clicked over and it was Dylan.

"I'm home early. Why am I alone?" he mused.

"I'm exhausted tonight. Tomorrow?" I asked. I heard Rocco bark in the background.

"She's coming over tomorrow night, buddy," Dylan said.

My stomach knotted at the disappointment in his voice. "I'll make it up to both of you."

"You will all night and the rest of your day off," Dylan said in a deep tone that made my stomach flutter.

"How were the games?"

"We lost today," he said and cursed. "But we're still ahead. We missed our lucky charm."

"I'm sorry. I'll be there for the next game—oh, wait, your next one is in Los Angeles?" I asked.

"Yeah. I've got news on that front too. Pollini wants me to read for the part of Gavin," he announced.

"That's great!" I exclaimed. We went on to discuss the ins and outs of the script. His enthusiasm was evident. He wanted this role, and I wanted it for him too.

"I want you there in Los Angeles with me so I can take you out no matter what happens," he said.

"Alright. I'll see if I can come," I said. "But I will

definitely be over tomorrow night. So it'll be late."

"I have no problem with taking you late," he said darkly.

My breath hitched. "I know."

"I want to take you out too, properly," he said.

I smiled. "I'd like that too, but I don't mind ordering in."

"You want my body," he half-joked.

"Not only, Dylan," I said.

"I know," he said just as quiet. "How are things at the theatre?" I told him everything, except about the *Les Misérables* audition. We discussed the Pollini script before ending.

I dropped my phone and covered my face with my hands. We were both going in different directions. Yet, I couldn't help the feelings I had for him. What was I going to do?

The door opened, with Gemma entering followed by West. They were singing "I Dream a Dream," from *Les Misérables* at the top of their lungs. I joined in with them. At first, it was humorous, but tonight I felt the song. They stopped singing, and I continued on alone.

My heart choked on the meaning and I fully committed myself to it, drawing on all of my failed auditions and losing the man I was falling in love with before we had a good chance to be together. Tears ran down my face as I poured everything I had into the moment. All the confusion, hope and loss soared out of me until I brought myself back.

Gemma and West broke into applause. "Oh, Brooke. You must go for the role of Fantine." She wiped a tear from the corner of her eye. "That was brilliant."

I smiled and did my cutesy twirl. "Thank you."

"I had no idea you could sing like that. I don't know why you aren't in *Les Misérables*," West said. "The tour auditions start in a couple of days. Are you auditioning?"

"Yes. We both are and we will get it," Gemma said confidently.

"Yeah, we will," I muttered. They talked me into a late takeout before I did my stretches and went to bed to prepare for the long day ahead. It was later than I intended, but I went to bed with the needed confidence that my acting break would come.

My early photo shoot and matinee show left me with little time to run back to my place, pack, and make it back to the theater in time for the evening show. Thankfully, I had Dylan's car service to help make it back in time and around the press that were still interested in Dylan and me as a couple.

By the time I finished and arrived at Dylan's building, I was tired again. Still, I felt a thrill go through me at seeing him again. Armed with a hoodie and dark glasses, I passed through the underground garage and entered the floor of his apartment. I was ready to fall asleep on arrival, but when Dylan came to the door with his eyes red-rimmed, I was instantly wide awake.

"Rocco's sick. The vet is in checking on him," he said.

I dropped my bag at the door and wrapped my

arms around his waist and he walked us back to where a middle age woman was on her knees examining Rocco. I could feel Dylan tense every time Rocco yelped and whined when she touched his stomach.

I ran my hand over his back. "It's going to be okay," I whispered.

"I'm going to take him back to the hospital and run some tests," the veterinarian said.

I dropped down and ran my hand over Rocco's soft head. I could feel Dylan's leg tremble and I rose back up to take his hand.

"I'll go with you," he said.

"Me too," I said to him.

He shook his head. "You look exhausted."

"Thanks for that," I teased and squeezed his hand. "You will not go alone. I'm coming with you. End of."

A soft smile appeared on his lips. "End of? You ordering me around?"

"For this I am," I said.

He brushed his lips against mine. "I can't argue right now. You can come along." I sighed and helped him get Rocco into his crate and we all moved down to cars in the parking garage, the two of us following her van out to the animal hospital. While we were driving, Dylan explained to me what had happened. "Rocco stopped eating today. The dog-sitter thought maybe it was because he missed me, but he was sick."

"We will find out and everything will be fine," I tried to assure him.

"It needs to be," Dylan said. He reached over and squeezed my knee. "Thank you for coming with me."

"Of course I would, always, even if we stopped what we're doing together. You can always call me if you need me," I said.

"The same for me, Brooke. I will always be there if you need me."

The animal hospital wasn't too far from his home, though we spent more time parking than getting inside. Dylan carried Rocco back and placed him down on the table before giving him a cuddle and leaving to go out with me to the waiting room. He pulled me to straddle his lap and hugged me like I was his favorite stuffed animal as we waited for her to run the test. After a couple of hours, the veterinarian came back out. "Rocco has an obstruction in his belly. It could be a meat bone he can't pass. It's a common surgery. He will need some looking after for a couple days here before returning him, but I do expect him to recover. I just need your permission to continue."

"You have it. Do whatever you need to do to make him better," Dylan told the vet. He finished up the paperwork and, the second he was done, had me back in his lap to hold on to until I drifted off to sleep. Sometime later, my phone buzzed with an incoming text from Gemma.

GemmaLvLy: The Les Misérables auditions are starting. Where are you?

Brooke. S: I'm not going to make the audition. Dylan needs me. His dog Rocco is in surgery. Go on. You got this!

GemmaLvLy: Alright. You'll get the next one. Talk 2U soon.

That was yet another thing I loved about Gemma. She accepted my answer and went on without questions. Dylan, on the other hand, wasn't as easy. He studied me. "What's going on?"

I shook my head and put on a smile. "Nothing. Let's just wait to hear about Rocco." I put my head back on his shoulder.

"We're not done with this conversation," he said. "You will tell me later."

"Yes, but later," I promised. He wrapped his arms back around me. More people came in to the hospital, but Dylan kept me where he had me. Finally, the doctor came out with an update. "He's fine, but I'll be keeping him for observation the rest of the week. You both can come back and see him."

I took Dylan's hand, and we went to the back and petted Rocco, who was still groggy. Dylan pinched tears away, and rubbed over his fur. "Don't you go nowhere, buddy."

Rocco licked his cheek, and I giggled. Dylan let him and kissed the top of his head.

I petted Rocco while he finished up with papers. Once we were done, he said to them, "I'll be…" He glanced back at me, and I nodded. "*We'll* be back to see him later. Call me with any changes." He took my hand, and we went out to the street.

"You need proper rest. We'll eat, fuck, and go to sleep," he said, then stopped and looked down at me. "Thank you... I need you with me. Will you stay longer?"

"I'm off work. I'm not leaving your side, and if you need me to come back after work tomorrow, I'm here."

He pulled me against his chest and kissed over my face. The flash of cameras brought us back to earth, and Dylan secured his glasses in place then mine before we made our way back to his car to head home. This time he parked, and took my hand and led me straight through the front door, stopping there to give me a passionate kiss. "I don't care, Brooke. I don't want to pretend anymore."

"We need to talk about this first," I cautioned, easing out of his arms and laughing it off for the cameras. He pressed his lips together but guided us inside the building.

When we reached his apartment, we showered and went back to his kitchen. He took out the food from yesterday and I helped him reheat the rice, steak, and Greek salad he had for us. "You have your career going and I have mine."

"I know that," he said.

I took a deep breath. "Today I had an audition for *Les Misérables* I missed."

"Why didn't you tell me?" He frowned.

"It was for a six-month traveling cast," I said.

His frown deepened. "Six months. Where?"

"All over the States, maybe abroad," I said and cut up my steak. "It would have meant you not seeing me for six months, and that's a problem. I didn't want to be without you for all that time." I wiped the stray tear from my eye.

He came around the island and put his hands on my hips and pressed his forehead against mine. "I don't want you going where I can't see you, but I would understand if it's for your career. I won't stand in the way of what works best for you. I want you to succeed. I'd have to do what I needed to do for my career."

I turned my head.

I had let my feelings come first. It wasn't just his need for me to stay with him, I had let my feelings come before my career, but Dylan wouldn't. Nicola had been right, when the time comes, he would move on. "I...understand, but it seems...we seem... I don't know. What are we doing?"

"We're dating," he said and kissed the tip of my nose.

I gave him an agreeing nod, though we ate the rest of our meal in silence.

We cleared everything away, and he came over to me and picked me up and moved us to his bedroom.

The door rang and Dylan checked the security monitor. It was Salvatore. I moved to hide, but Dylan took my arm. "Whoever it is will have to deal with it."

I nodded, and he answered. Salvatore walked in and, when he saw me, the smile left his face. "Brooke. You're..."

"Dating me for real," Dylan said. "We can handle it."

Salvatore glared at me. "This ends your contract."

I cleared my throat. "I don't want to be paid to date Dylan."

I could feel Dylan's eyes on me. "We will keep her fees going and she can do some of my publicity outreach for organizations instead of being paid for dating me."

"I've got my show, stagehand work, and Colby's on the weekends. I'll be fine," I said.

"I'll be speaking with Raymond," Salvatore said icily.

"So will I," I told him.

"She gets fired or let go, I walk," Dylan said in annoyance.

"She's not fired, but I suppose it doesn't matter now. I stopped by to tell you that Pollini will be there personally for your audition!" he said excitedly.

"Thank you, but that could have been a phone call. Stop dropping by my place. You're not my fucking chaperone." He closed the door behind Salvatore, who promptly left and, from the set of his shoulders, I knew this wasn't the end of it. Dylan ignored him and lifted me in his arms.

I smiled though my stomach knotted. "Angry sex?"

"Not this time, beautiful," he replied.

I stiffened in his arms as he carried me back into the bedroom.

Placing me down on the bed, he stretched out, facing me, his finger stroking under my chin. "Why don't you want me to be tender with you?"

I averted my eyes. "Will my explaining make you change your mind?" I replied, answering a question with a question. I always hated when people did that.

"No," he admitted and tugged my shirt up over my stomach and glanced down at my pussy. "But you will tell me why."

I squeezed my eyes shut, hating myself for how turned on I was by him and how weak I felt in wanting him to touch me. "It was just the situation with Salvatore and Raymond. I feel out of my depth."

"So you wanted me to fuck you hard and that will make you forget?" he asked, but from his tone I could tell he knew I was lying to him.

He sighed heavily and took off our clothes, then

hugged me to him. "You have nothing to worry about. I promise I'll take care of it… I'll take care of you. Let me show you."

The rough caress of his day's growth beard brushed my skin as he nuzzled into my neck and breathed me in. "I'm glad you're here with me."

My heart soared. I buried my hands deep in his hair and kissed his forehead, "There's nowhere else I'd rather be."

He moved his head back and looked directly at me. There went my racing pulse and that fluttering I got under his stare, but this time I found something else. Something that made fear almost overwhelm the sensual moment.

My emotions went into overload. Had I given away too much of my true feelings? Did he know how much he had come to mean to me?

Dylan broke our contact first with a kiss, delving his tongue between my lips and sliding it against my own. It heated me all the way down to my swelling clit that pulsed between my thighs as desire for him filled me.

I squirmed in his arms, but Dylan calmly continued to kiss me, letting me know he was in control. He would dominate our pleasure, and that made me hotter. I surrendered and kissed him back with all the feelings I had for him.

My breasts were swollen by the time he reached for them. And when he did, I arched my back and rubbed over his hair as I watched pleasure fill his face while he suckled them.

Groaning, Dylan let go of my breasts and captured my lips again in a deep, passionate kiss. He spread me wider as he kissed his way down to my mound. The throbbing ache there surged. I needed him to soothe it.

"Please," I whispered.

"I've got you," he said as he spread my thighs, his mouth descending between them. I balled the sheets in my fists as he kissed my pussy, lapping through the slick folds and swirling his tongue around my clit, every brush of his tongue heightening the sensations. I could feel my orgasm building. He crooked a finger inside as he relentlessly licked and sucked me. Knowing my body, he stroked his finger over my spot until I came with a cry on my lips as pleasure flowed through me.

I was still coming when his thick, hard cock eased inside me. I felt a glorious clench of my sex as he ground his cock against my clit. Pleasure coursed through me as he moved faster and deeper. I clasped his muscular shoulders tightly. I didn't ever want it to stop.

"Dylan," I cried out.

"I can't get enough of you," he said with a growl. He was back down between my thighs, sucking on my clit. Pleasure overloaded my nerve endings as he reignited my orgasm and I screamed. White light crossed my vision as I rose up from the mattress.

I didn't think I could take any more, but he moved back on top of me and thrust deep inside me again. I whimpered.

"Stay with me, Brooke."

Swiveling his hips, he ground his cock in deeper than he ever had before. Every inch of him sent shocks of ecstasy coursing through my body. Sweat covered our skin as we moved against each other.

Grasping the sides of his face, I softly cried, "Dylan."

Our gazes locked as he began short, hard thrusts. The rhythmic strokes of his cock brought me close again. I felt my body stiffening and tightening once more.

"Oh. Fuck, Brooke," he groaned.

My flesh tightened around him until I convulsed again in his arms as he came with me. His whole powerful body shuddered while my inner walls gripped and spasmed around his cock.

Taking my mouth again, he kissed me as we rode out our blissful climaxes. This was more than I ever experienced before. I was ecstatically drained of energy. My heart swelled in my chest when he finally placed me in what had become my resting place against his chest, bonding us even closer together.

I held in the tears as I pressed my lips over his heart that was beating hard, expressing how much it meant for the way he had just made love to me. *Love.* I had completely and utterly fallen in love with him.

CHAPTER
SEVENTEEN

Dylan

I kissed Brooke's forehead before easing her off the top of me so as not to wake her, while I went to make a call to the animal hospital to check on Rocco. He had made it through the night and was looking good on recovery from the surgery. If he hadn't, I didn't know what I'd have done. But I wasn't alone with my worries—Brooke stayed with me. She was alright, the way she kept encouraging me, telling me he was going to be fine. She carried me through all those hours and I couldn't thank her enough. But I didn't know she'd missed an audition for me. Why hadn't she said anything? Of course I was gutted when I found out. Hell, I'd be gutted if she left for six months. But I wasn't selfish enough to keep her from a chance at success.

It hurt to see Brooke struggle. She worked hard to get her acting career off. I was fortunate to have a leg up. Even with the tabloids following me, they kept my name alive, though it almost made me notorious. Since I'd been with Brooke, they eased up and now I'd been offered a Pollini script. I was chuffed when Salvatore broke the news. Working with Pollini had the potential to rocket my acting career. It wasn't a chance I could refuse. And if I got my due, I would do whatever I could to help Brooke move up too.

I slumped down on my couch and wiped my hand over my face.

Where were all these feelings coming from? I didn't know how she had become so important to me so fast. But she was and I honestly wasn't sure how I felt about it. I had thought the right step would be to date her, but even that wasn't what was happening. It felt like a relationship. Something I wasn't ready for. Sure I enjoyed being with her, but I didn't want to hurt her. We had somehow jumped ahead before we had a chance to properly get to know each other. Was it too late to slow down?

I just needed some time on my own to think.

"Dylan, what're you doing out here?" Brooke appeared, wearing one of my T-shirts. She looked beautiful all tussled, her eyes darting over my face trying to read me. "I was checking on Rocco. He's fine. I've got a lot of things to do today."

I got up and walked past her, over to the refrigerator, and snagged a bottle of water. "Do you want one?" I glanced at her.

She was looking down at her toes, and my stomach muscles knotted. "No... uhm. Well, since you're busy, I should probably go. I'll stop at the vets and see Rocco before I leave the area, if that's okay."

Fuck, was she a sweetheart. Now I felt like shite. It hurt me to treat her that way. I wouldn't. "You can stay here, Brooke. We can go back to sleep and go later. I can take you back before practice."

"Do you really want that, Dylan?" Brooke showing me her vulnerable side hit me right in the chest. It turned me on too. I adjusted myself.

Away from her, I could say "no," but when she was with me, I didn't want her to leave. Her lingering looks and kisses over my heart after we had sex made it clear enough she was into me. I was being selfish. Even now, I couldn't stop myself from going over and pulling her up in my arms and carrying her back to bed. "I do."

That was how it had gone for the rest of the week. When I was brooding about Rocco still staying in the hospital, she got me out to shop for stuff Rocco didn't need. My flat had become a pet palace, with bright, colorful toys everywhere, but I didn't mind. As Brooke put it, 'it gave it character.'"

My real reason for doing it was that I was getting off on how much it made her happy. Her joy was addictive. I craved it when she wasn't around. And at the same time, fearing it when she was. She kept on with me and, in a way, showed how easy it could be for us, if we were in a relationship instead of just dating.

Rocco's surgery was a success and after a week, Brooke was right there with me to bring him home. We continued to spoil him rotten around New York City. The press was eating it up. Someone had created an Instagram of Rocco around town. He was getting thousands of hits. I didn't mind the pictures because some of them captured Brooke and me together, and not one appeared unhappy. It was all true. I was happy with her.

She'd meet me after her jobs and classes to do lines with the Pollini script. Neither one of us talked about what it would mean if I got the role. I'd have to leave. But Brooke had my back. I even got her to go see the acting coach I used, and he was impressed by her, too. She had what it took, and I wanted to see her as successful as she had made me. I got her some sessions with him to use on her own time. She fussed about it, but I wasn't having it. I wanted to give her any advantage she could get in the acting business. The more time I spent with Brooke, the more it seemed like we were in a relationship. It was all confusing.

Whilst I thought on it all, I called a meeting at my apartment with Salvatore and Nicola to discuss what I could do for Brooke since we had broken the agreement. Normally, I would have tried my accountant, but Salvatore and Nicola were great at helping me build my life here in the United States. I was sure they would be helpful with Brooke. I knew Nicola had spoken to Raymond about our relationship and he was waiting on a new contract from me. I had put it off, but it was over two weeks since Sal dropped in and we told him. They were pressuring me to address it. What I was sure of was that I wanted to continue to help Brooke in any way I could.

They were at my apartment on time, Nicola attempting to kiss my lips when I leaned in to kiss her cheek. I shook my head at her, but she laughed. Salvatore's face was blank when he took a seat across from me on the couch.

"Everything is working. New York is willing to work around your schedule, should the filming start before the five-and-a-half months," Nicola said.

"If I get the part," I added.

"The audition is a technicality. We have worked with Raymond on contacts and places to arrange in Los Angeles, unless you want to live in Malibu?" Salvatore asked.

"I don't know. Did you schedule your meeting with Raymond about Brooke?" I asked.

They glanced between them. Nicola spoke first. "We got your proposal, but we don't see any reason to continue paying Ms. Sullivan. It would be seen as highly inappropriate. She is working."

"Yes, she's in the play, but I don't want to leave her without income. I want a special fund set up for her. I'd like you to double the amount she was originally paid. We could add her to all of my charity promotions," I said.

"Dylan, that's a bit excessive…" Nicola said.

I shrugged. "I don't believe it is, and I'd like for you to find out about other promotional opportunities we can make her a part of. Salvatore, you have contacts?"

Salvatore's smile tightened. "I don't know where to start with Ms. Sullivan. I mean, you never did anything like that with the other…ladies you were seeing. I mean, the charities already decided on you as their spokesperson. It would take much more than a phone call from me or you to decide on Brooke. There would need to be some protocol. She can be seen with you like we originally planned."

I folded my arms. "I've seen you do it before. If it's an

issue, I'll call them myself."

"That's not necessary," Nicola said quickly. "Salvatore and I will do our best by Ms. Sullivan, but we will ask you to try to focus on the script and preparation for Los Angeles. This is an enormous opportunity that a line of A-list actors would clamor for the chance at."

"Yes. Let us take care of Ms. Sullivan," Salvatore said. "I'll schedule a meeting with Raymond soon and we will present her with a new contract."

"Thank you," I said. "Thank you both." We went over more together and I signed a few agreements before they rose to leave. Salvatore was out the door before Nicola, who stopped at the entryway. "Are you thinking of having Ms. Sullivan come with you to Los Angeles, not just for the game, but when you move there permanently?" Her tone was light, but the vein on her forehead jumped as she waited for my answer.

I stared off. "I'm not moving to Los Angeles right now. No, I haven't planned for her to come with me. I haven't thought about it."

Her shoulders dropped and she smiled. "I didn't think so, but I thought to ask. Leave Ms. Sullivan in our hands and we will take care of everything for your transition. Congrats on the Pollini invitation, Dylan. This is a huge step in your career as an actor."

I didn't feel like celebrating. It felt wrong.

"Thanks," I muttered and closed the door.

I had to shake this shitty feeling I had. What else could I do right now? We weren't ready for more. Right? Fuck. I hated how indecisive this had made me. My head was messed up. I needed some time by myself. Changing into my shorts and trainers, I grabbed my ear buds and left my flat for a run.

Just as I entered Central Park, my phone vibrated in my pocket. It was Brooke. A weirdness filled my chest as I looked down at her photo I had saved to the phone. She was probably interested in what happened during our meeting. Or was offering to go with me to pick up Rocco from his checkup. I still wanted her to do those things, but would it be fair in the end? Would she move her life around for me? Did I want her to do that?

We needed some distance, so I could get some perspective. It was the only way to stop from making what was happening between us more than I was ready for right now.

Sighing heavily, I turned off my phone and returned to my run.

CHAPTER
EIGHTEEN

Brooke

I dragged myself up the stairs to my apartment from an on-call evening shift at Colby's on Sunday. The happy disposition had left me drained by the end of the shift—that, along with the lack of contact with Dylan. I hadn't seen much of him over the last week. Sure, he had been at practice in preparation for the New York Football Club's away matches with LA Galaxy that was set to happen in Los Angeles in a couple of days.

As for myself, I had been busy too with rehearsals. When he did come over, it was late at night for sex and sleep. The sex was great, and I loved the feel of waking up in his arms or watching him open his eyes in the morning. But watching him leave left me feeling empty. I didn't know how to approach him about it, so I hadn't yet.

Opening the door, I was met by Gemma bouncing up from her seat on the couch and screaming, "I'm Cosette in the tour of *Les Misérables*."

My energy spiked up with her news and I screamed, "Oh, my God!" and ran over and hugged her. "Don't forget me when you become a big star." Truly, I was happy for her, but it also meant I was going to have to find a new roommate.

She kissed both my cheeks. "Never."

I clasped my hands together. "We should celebrate." We plopped down on the couch. Gemma turned to me and asked, "I thought you were seeing Dylan tonight?"

I lifted my brows. "I don't know." She put her arm around my shoulder. "Something happen?"

"No... I don't know," I stammered.

She frowned. "If it isn't working, break it off with him."

I bit into my lip. "It's working...it's just he's been busy." I took out my phone and fiddled with it. "I'll call him about going out tonight." The voicemail icon was lit. It was Raymond's number. I stopped to play it first.

Ray. WTS: I'd like to meet with you before the new contract meeting tomorrow.

I ran my hand over my sour stomach.

"Something wrong?" Gemma asked.

"Raymond wants to meet with me before our meeting," I replied.

Her lips parted and her breath hissed out. Early meetings with Raymond weren't usually good news. Gemma still didn't know the ins and outs of the agreement, only that it provided some promotional work that was working out well up until now. "What did Dylan tell you?"

"He said the meeting was a technicality," I said.

"Then that's what you think until told something different," she proclaimed. "Don't get down. I want you out to celebrate. Call him. I'd like a fancy, ridiculously indulgent dinner, where we can dress up and get waiters to put cloths in our laps."

I giggled and texted Dylan.

Brooke.S.: Gemma got a lead part in Les Miz! Are you up for going out to celebrate?

Dylan M. Pierce: I'm with Knox. He's keen. You want him to come along?

I scrunched up my face. He knew I didn't, but Gemma was waiting, so I told her, "He's with Knox."

"Oh? Good. Tell him he can come along," she said.

I lowered my brows. "Gemma, from what I heard from Dylan, he's kind of a slut."

She shrugged. "So is Dylan and you're out with him?"

"But...we're dating now, exclusively," I said. "I don't want you to get hurt by Knox."

She laughed heartily at that. "I don't want to keep him. I'd shag him for a few hours and he can go right on back to..."

"Slutsville?" I said, and we laughed together. "I'm not serious. I can handle myself," she said.

I wasn't convinced, but I texted Dylan back and they agreed to pick us up. We went to our rooms, and I took out a black wraparound dress and sandals, then took a shower and changed into them. I was adding curls to my hair when Gemma walked in. She was all dolled up with her blonde hair back in a high ponytail and a gray shimmer mini-dress and stilettos. She joined me in the mirror at the back of my closet door and said, "How do I look?"

My eyes widened. Gemma was never insecure. "You look stunning. He will fall at your feet."

"I want dinner first," she half-joked. "I don't know why I'm nervous. I don't usually go for the pretty-boy type, but, well…"

"You'll be fine," I assured her. The door buzzed. "I told them not to come up." I motioned around to the disaster that had become my room, and was sure Gemma's was just as untidy.

"Alright, love." She linked arms with me and we headed outside.

My heartbeat sped up at the sight of Dylan coming closer to me. He was dressed in a button-down shirt, blazer and dress pants. His blond hair was up in an intricate knot that looked complicated and hot as hell. He came over to me and kissed my lips. "You look beautiful."

"So do you," I said, and he took my hand. "You scrub up well, eh, Gemma?" he teased her.

"I was thinking you only owned shorts," she said back to him.

Knox came around the car, looking good too. He was dressed in a fancy, fitted V-neck, a blazer, and pants. The diamonds in his ears shone as bright as the smile his green-eyed gaze had on Gemma's breasts. Unlike me, she didn't mind. In fact, she arched, giving him a better look. It wasn't until he moved real close to her that Gemma took a step back and laughed a little.

He smiled down at her. "I've been trying to get you out for the last month."

"Is that so." I turned my head away from the stink-eyes directed at me. "My fault. I didn't want anything to get weird."

"I'm never weird," Gemma said.

"Neither am I," Knox said and took her hand and kissed the back of it. "You ready, beautiful? We'll go wherever you want to go tonight."

"We already made reservations at Allegro," Dylan said.

"Allegro?" Gemma said and smiled at me. Only the most exclusive eatery in town. "That'll work."

Dylan placed his hand on my butt and moved me to the car. "We can get takeout."

"They don't do takeout," I fussed.

"It was a joke," Dylan said once we were in the car. Gemma and Knox got in, and we rode to the restaurant.

The restaurant had a line, but we were able to walk right in and were seated at a table centrally located in the minimalist styled dining room. Several phones came out around us to take photos of Dylan and Knox, but they acted oblivious to the attention. We ordered the chef's sample dinner and a bottle of wine, which they brought right away.

The conversation flowed as did the wine, from subjects of soccer, to theater and movies.

"The original *Total Recall* is the best movie ever made," Knox proclaimed.

Dylan and I both laughed at Gemma's expression.

"Ever? Are you serious?" she asked him.

"Yes. I watch it every time it's on. It has everything in it. Action, suspense, a hot chick and humor. What more could you want?" he explained. "Come on, back me up, brother."

"Yep. The best," Dylan said, and they shared some male bonded laughter. The waitress came over with our next entree and Knox gave her an ogle that had her blushing. She passed a card to him and he tucked it in his jacket. I glared at him and over at Gemma, who appeared to take it in stride as we silently ate our meal. But I knew better. She was hurt.

"What is your favorite movie?" Dylan asked me to revive the conversation as he finished off his glass of wine.

"*The Red Shoes*," I said between bites of my salad.

He and Knox gave me a blank stare, and I told them a brief synopsis. "It changed everything. I wanted to be a ballerina."

Gemma giggled. "Me too, but that wasn't my favorite."

Knox leaned close to her. "What is your favorite?"

"Baloo," she said.

I giggled. "Baloo? You mean *The Jungle Book*. I thought *Pulp Fiction* was your favorite…"

Dylan frowned, and I turned to watch Baloo charge over to the table.

"I got your message, Gemma," he said. We all turned to her.

"I checked in on social media and sent a text. I didn't think he'd come," she said, but I could tell she did. "Why don't you join us?"

"Like hell he can," Knox said.

I gave Gemma a pointed look. "Don't do this, Gemma. Baloo, you should go home."

"Gemma, if you want to go home. It's okay. I've got my car and I'll take you," Baloo said.

Gemma's face turned pink, but she rose and walked over to Baloo's side. "I'll go talk with him. Excuse me."

"Gemma," I scolded. This was dramatic and impulsive for Gemma. She hadn't even coordinated a good excuse with Baloo.

"You're coming back," Knox said. It came out more as an order than a question. Either way, Gemma didn't answer. She just walked out with Baloo.

Knox turned to me. "What the hell?"

"I'm sorry. She probably won't come back," I cautioned. "So we may as well go on with our meal."

"She'd better fucking come back," Knox growled. "That's rude."

When the third meal sampler came out, Knox had had enough and threw down his napkin and stormed out.

Dylan tut-tutted. "What the fuck was that? I thought better of Gemma."

"Knox was eye-humping the waitress. I don't blame Gemma for saving face," I snipped. "It was wrong to leave with Baloo, but she probably didn't think Knox would care either way."

"So you thought this Baloo guy would show up?" Dylan asked, his tone sharp. "And what kind of fucking name is Baloo?"

I scoffed. "His name, and I like it. I didn't know he would come, but I don't blame Gemma one bit for leaving with him. Knox will learn to make his own dates on his own time."

"He was just being polite," he said and lifted up Knox's napkin. A card dropped out. "Gemma stirred up drama."

My purse buzzed with an incoming message from Gemma.

GemmaLvLy: Back at ours. Sorry, but I couldn't stay. Apologize to everyone. A rain check for Knox if he wants one.

Dylan's lips pressed together. "What did it say?"

I shrugged and shared Gemma's message.

He snorted. "Rain check? Is she daft? She was rude. He's done."

I narrowed my gaze. "She not daft. He was rude to her too. He was on a date with her."

"It wasn't a real date," Dylan said. "It was a meal and a fuck—"

"So you set my friend up for a meal-fuck? Even if she was interested, she still deserves better than being mistreated at the restaurant. I don't care if he did get rid of the card, he should have shown her some respect. Fuck Knox," I said hotly.

"Fuck Gemma. He was being polite, but he didn't want her getting any ideas. What is it with you women?" Dylan said.

"So now it's 'you women'? You throwing me in there too? I expect too much too, because I've fallen…" *I've fallen in love with you.* I clamped my hands over my mouth and my pulse went into overdrive.

His brows knitted. "You've what?"

I shook my head. I couldn't finish saying it. Didn't he know what I meant?

He blew out his breath. Reaching his hand over to mine, he took my hand, then nodded toward the other tables. "Let's continue talking about this some other time. You want to come over?"

My stomach knotted. "No. I think I want to go back to my place and see Gemma. I have the meeting in the morning anyway and I need to finish packing for L.A. if I'm going to your LA Galaxy game and plan to be there for your audition tomorrow."

"Okay, if that's what you want," he said. We quietly ate the rest of the meal, then settled the bill and I called my own car.

He got in next to me and said, "We have early morning practice. I will be speaking with them before your meeting, but I will meet you at the airport."

I nodded, and he pecked my lips before I got out in front of my building.

Once I was inside, the car pulled off. My heart was heavy with worry. Could Dylan ever love, or see a future with, me?

CHAPTER

NINETEEN

"I 'd like to hear your side before we meet with them," Raymond said as I sat across from him in his office. He had offered to meet with me fifteen minutes before to hear my side of the story. I didn't have any explanation besides the truth.

"It happened recently. We hadn't planned it," I said.

"How long?" he asked.

"After our first jog outing," I replied.

He scoffed. "You should have told me."

I ran my hands down the front of my skirt. "I didn't know where our attraction would go. It just means the relationship—I mean, dating—is real now. We both believe we can maintain our professionalism."

"I understand, Brooke, and I believe you. However, Dylan has a pattern of singling out the women that worked with him, then breaking up badly with them. This was the exact situation his team wanted to avoid. That was the reason I recommended, and they hired, you." His disappointment was evident in his voice.

I lowered my head. "I understand that and I apologize for putting you in this awkward situation. It happened and we can only go on from here. We are still a couple in public. I don't see how this can't still go forward. I'm fine with not getting paid."

"And you think you can afford to do that?" He exhaled. "Brooke, you know that job at *Rent* was temporary—"

"Temporary? You said a few weeks ago that my part had a chance at being permanent." I interjected.

"Yes, but you know how things change and the second I was sure it had, I called you in early." He sighed. "I hadn't wanted to tell you yet, but my friend over there said they are discussing having Dahlia Wood join the cast for a limited run. It would be temporary, but that would move you off the cast. They may have a day open for stagehand work, but that's it."

My lips parted. "I lost *Rent*. How soon?"

"Sooner than telling them you want no money," he replied. "I know you are upset, but you have to think practically."

A knock on the door ended our conversation, and his assistant held it open for Salvatore and Nicola. Both were in power suits today. They shook hands professionally with the both of us before taking the seats next to me.

Nicola spoke first. "Your client deceived us and created a relationship with Dylan behind our back. We could by right request all sums and money and additional fees for her violation of the contract."

The blood drained from my face and I looked at Raymond. He held up his hand. "This would involve both parties."

"Yes, but the bottom line is the terms of the original agreement have changed and we'd like to terminate it immediately. We are prepared to offer a small severance package that should help your client over the next month. However," —she opened her case— "we are prepared to extend the severance package to three months provided that your client agrees to end contact after the Los Angeles game."

My stomach churned. "I'm being contracted to not contact Dylan? But we're dating. He never mentioned breaking up with me."

"He never does," Nicola said meeting my eyes. "But believe me Dylan is breaking up with you. He told me as much. This meeting is to help you. He does...consider you a friend. He'd like to make the transition easy, as he has done for all his other...ladies."

"What?" My eyes widened. "Dylan didn't mention any of this last night. I'll call him—"

"No, you mustn't," Nicola said cutting me off. "We just finished speaking with Dylan. He is preparing for the game. He told us to speak with you. There is nothing said today that he doesn't know about."

"We have gone over every part of this with him. We'd prefer not to get him... upset before the game," Salvatore added. "This is Dylan's usual pattern, which I tried to warn you about." His tone was curt. He cleared his throat. "As Raymond is aware, there is a ninety-nine percent chance he will be getting the role in Los Angeles with

Pollini, not to mention many other obligations that would lead him out of New York City."

"Salvatore's right," Nicola said. "He has the Pollini meeting when he arrives in L.A. and the game to contend with. It wouldn't have been in the agreement if he didn't want it there. He told me himself, he's not taking you with him when he moves to Los Angeles after he ends his soccer contract. He told us you were a good mate, but things between you have gotten too serious. He wasn't ready for a relationship. Therefore, he wanted to make sure you were well taken care of."

I pursed my lips. Dylan discussed our relationship with them? It was a betrayal I couldn't easily digest, but what she said did sound like what had happened between us. It had happened fast, so fast that he had pulled away from me over the last few days. And after last night, when there was no doubt he knew I had almost professed loving him, he had ignored it and quickly sought to end the evening. Truly, I had gotten too close. He always said this wasn't going to end in flowers and romance. Still, this didn't seem like the Dylan I knew, but they had known him longer. I just couldn't believe it, but what other choice did I have but to accept it?

I took a deep breath and looked at Raymond. "What do you think?"

"Salvatore is right about Dylan leaving for filming. He was clear on his goal to move to Los Angeles. We have had discussions with Pollini's people. He will get offered the role," Raymond confirmed.

"Actually, we met with him before you. The audition is a mere technicality," Salvatore said and glanced at me.

"Dylan is likely to be moving to Los Angeles soon. You must understand as an actress, this opportunity is his big break."

Nicola smiled. "We are in negotiations to end the New York City Football Club contract after his meeting in Los Angeles for the movie. You haven't known Dylan that long. Salvatore and I have known him for years. Dylan wouldn't want to leave you completely without some... help."

"He's offering to let you do some future publicity shots for his Children and Families in Need charity, which is also in the new contract," Nicola said. "As long as you maintain good character, this would be good work and publicity for you."

"Yes, good publicity," Salvatore echoed. "You're not getting married, you had a few dates. I'm sure you can date someone else." They quieted and waited for my answer.

"I don't want to use the foundation," I finally spoke. "But I won't be a conflict in his way of getting his big break. Dylan doesn't need me to go to the Los Angeles game today. I'll go home."

"He's counting on you being there to support him at his audition. He's expecting you there and the information has already been leaked to the press you would be there," Salvatore said. "Surely you don't want to mess up his big day? Going with him is the professional thing to do after you broke the agreement. Raymond, please back me up on this?"

"Brooke, this is the best way ahead," Raymond said.

I took a deep breath. I didn't know how they could

expect me to go, but from their point of view I had broken my agreement. To them this was all about a job on which I behaved unprofessionally, not about what Dylan and I shared. It didn't sound like Dylan at all, but how long had I actually known him? Why he wanted me there made no sense. I believed us to be friends. I wouldn't ruin his big day, but I didn't want anything else from him. "I will never mess up Dylan's opportunity. I don't need the money."

"Wait," Raymond said, "I'll speak with my client alone."

"We'll need an answer, now," Nicola said.

Raymond's brows lifted. He looked at me. "Think of your new promotions."

He didn't say much, but what he said was enough. I wouldn't be able to afford his fees for the job or pay for the remainder of the Q Studios without it. But that wasn't the reason for my agreeing. I wanted Dylan to succeed and get everything he wanted. They were right, I was the only one in this relationship conflicted.

"Yes," I cleared my throat. "I understand. But for what it's worth, I do care about Dylan. I want the best for him. I can't help I fell in love with him."

Nicola bristled and Salvatore gave me a sorrowful look.

"However, I will not stand in the way of his career. He doesn't need to get a contract together to get rid of me, but since this is how he arranges things with the two of you, I'll sign," I choked.

"Great," Salvatore replied in relief. "Sorry this happened to you and we understand you are upset, but we'll need you to maintain your professionalism. Dylan doesn't want you discussing this meeting when we meet up with him."

"Salvatore is right. He has a game and a big audition. He needs to keep positive things in his head. I could get Dylan to give you a bonus to help cover the cost of your additional work for us today," Nicola said.

My eyes stung. "Just give me a minute."

I left the room and rushed over to the bathroom and splashed cold water on my tear-stained face. My phone rang with an image of Dylan with Rocco that I had taken when Rocco came out of the hospital. His carefree joy caused a lump to form in my throat. I read his message and sent my own.

Dylan M. Pierce: You go over everything with Nicola and Salvatore and sign the new contract?

My stomach flipped over. This was his idea all along.

Brooke S.: Yes. I'll see you at the airport.

I went back into the room and signed the papers.

"If you need a ride…" Salvatore said.

"No, thank you," I replied coolly, and the two of them left. I sank down in the chair.

"Something will come in, I promise you. You just need to hold on a little longer," Raymond said to me.

Hold on a little longer. The words echoed through my head as I looked at the window. My mind mulled over the countless times I had heard as much from him over the past couple of years. Every time I picked myself back up and put myself back out there, I'd watched everyone I'd known move on ahead of me. "Thank you for helping me over these two years."

"That sounds ominous. You take a break, regroup. I promise I'll be in touch soon," he said.

I didn't answer. I no longer had an answer. Therefore, I did the only thing I could do. I left.

I arrived at the airport, spotted Kayla and waved.

"How good to see you again. Have you been to L.A. before?" she asked.

"Yes, with my parents, but not often," I said. We were moving toward the gate when Tyler came running up to greet us. "May I please speak with Brooke a minute?"

"It's okay. I'll catch up with you," I replied.

He licked his lips. "I'm sorry. I was drunk at the party. I was out of order."

I waved my hand. "No worries. It's over."

"I know you're with Dylan now," he said, his voice going up at the end.

I stared at him in puzzlement. *Does he know? Probably not.* I turned my head and responded, "We're together."

"Okay," he drew out. We walked quietly toward the gate.

"I heard you were in a show. My little sister, Zoe, is in the ballet," he said.

I smiled. "Really? I took ballet when I was younger."

He grinned and we chatted the rest of the way to the

gate. He told me about his growing up in New Jersey and his sister's experience in the New York Ballet. As it turned out, sober Tyler wasn't too bad, especially when he talked about his sister. The conversation was a distraction, but I couldn't stop thinking about Dylan. I wanted Dylan.

"Brooke."

A shiver raced up my spine at the sound of Dylan calling my name. When I turned and saw him, he opened his arms wide for me to fill them. A part of me wanted to rush over, but my mind was still reeling from all the things said in the meeting with Salvatore and Nicola. But this was a part of our public persona, and a role I had agreed to play civilly to the end of my contract. Besides, I was happy for his big audition and wouldn't dream of doing anything to upset his chances.

Hastening my pace, I went into his arms and he wrapped them around me and kissed me possessively. When we ended the kiss, he asked. "What are you doing chatting with him?"

"He apologized. That's all," I said, watching Tyler move away.

"That's enough," he said.

Placing his hand on the center of my back, he led us through security and on to the plane where we rode in business class with the team. The two of us looked over his script. After a couple of hours, I cuddled up next to him and slept the remainder of the flight, savoring the feel of his arms for all the time I had left.

We arrived and rode with Nicola and Salvatore straight over to Pollini's private office in Santa Monica for his audition. My stomach turned over at the tension in the car, but the ride was short and before I knew it we were all grouping before the glass building.

"Brooke, you can stay in the car," Nicola said once we were on the sidewalk.

"She will go in," Dylan said. His tone curt. He took my hand and kissed the back of it. "She can wait outside the office. I want to see her the second the meeting finishes."

"It would be highly inappropriate," Nicola protested.

"She can wait in the lobby," Salvatore offered.

"I'm fine in the lobby," I agreed.

I gave him the thumbs-up as they went to check in and disappeared in the elevators to the fortieth floor. Once they were gone, I deflated and went outside to get some cool air. My phone rang with a call from my mother.

"Hello, darling. I saw in your email you might be coming to Seattle with the soccer team?" She hesitated over the words "soccer team."

"No... Not sure," I stammered.

"Something happen?" she asked.

"Yeah, but I'll be fine," I said in a small voice.

"You sure? Do you need money?" She muffled the phone.

"I knew it," I heard my father say. They argued before his voice came on the phone line. "You've done your best and gave it a good try, but you are almost up to year three. How many years do you have left to become a working actress? Two? It's a career for the young."

"I'm acting in..." I was about to say *Rent*, but I now knew that was ending. "I'm not ready to—"

"I can compromise," he said. "There's a studio space downtown. You were always good at ballet. If you want,

I can give you a loan to start your own dance studio for youths. You could still act occasionally in town and stay with us until you get on your feet. What do you say?"

"I… I don't know," I stuttered.

It wasn't an offer to easily refuse. I could still do something in my art, just have more stability.

"Stubborn," he grumbled.

"Just like you," I heard my mother yell in the background.

"I'll think on it," I agreed.

"Good. Here's your mother," he said, and she returned to the line.

"You will?" she asked. "What about your dating Dylan Pierce?"

I glanced up at the door and the bright smile on Dylan's face as he came for me. "I'll tell you soon. I must go." I hung up the phone.

He picked me up in a hug and spun me around. "I got the part!"

"Of course you did," I said excitedly. "Salvatore and Nicola?"

"They are up there discussing negotiations with his team. I need to get to the field for the game," he said.

We got in the car and headed off to the stadium. "I'm going to take you out to celebrate tonight."

"Actually, I'm really tired," I replied.

He frowned and pressed his lips against my forehead. "You don't feel warm. Alright. I'll take care of you when I get back."

I forced a smile and nodded. "So tell me all that happened?" I asked with a lift in my voice.

Dylan told me all that Pollini had shared so far. They would have a slew of meetings in California over the next couple of months before filming.

"So will you be moving to Los Angeles soon?" I asked. Even though Salvatore and Nicola had told me, I had hoped to hear as much from him anyway.

He chewed his lip. "Not right away. I still have a good five months on my contract, but Nicola is negotiating reduced games."

"Oh. I see," I said and looked down at my shaking hands.

"We'll work it out," he said and kissed the side of my head. "You will still be busy with *Rent*?"

I shook my head. "No. Raymond's meeting said I will not be kept on the permanent cast."

"I'm sorry," he said sympathetically. "But something else will come along soon. I'm sure. If you have time free, you can fly out to L.A. I was thinking of taking a break after the Seattle game."

I plastered on a smile. "Probably not, since I'll have to look for more work, but honestly this is a huge opportunity. You won't need to fly in your sex-buddy."

"Sex-buddy? We're dating," he said. "I'd call that more than a sex buddy."

I lowered my eyelids. "Of course." We both stared out our windows into busy, though moving, traffic. Dylan's hand ran down my arm and that flare of connection we shared brought back my awareness of him. "Come closer."

I scooted across the leather seat, and he put his arm around me.

"That's better," he muttered.

I bit the inside of my cheek. I didn't trust my response so I let him hold me the rest of the way to the StubHub Center. He had a game. Our last game together.

I didn't have time to think about it.

Once the car pulled up at the entrance, the press and a sea of fans were already there. And though it was a gated-off area, it was a catwalk to the entrance that was lined with people on either side. It was thrilling as well as intimidating, but nonetheless our path to the stadium. We still had our public image, and I followed Dylan's lead. He took my hand, and we got out. I smiled and patiently waited while he signed a few autographs before moving slowly forward. When we got next to the doors, he stopped us and all cameras pointed our way. There he gripped me by the waist and leaned his forehead against mine. The press loved it. The flashes were going off like fireworks. "I've got to go. I'll be looking for you at the end of the game."

"I'll be there," I rasped.

He kissed me, then took my hand, and we went inside the building. We moved forward down a hallway that forked, one leading to the private entrance for the teams. Dylan gave me a wave before disappearing, while I was led over to a short flight of stairs to the VIP section in the stands. I immediately spotted Kayla in her team jersey and hugged her in greeting before taking the empty seat next to her.

"Are you staying the rest of the week?" she asked.

I shook my head. "No I… I have a few things to do. I'll be leaving after the game."

Her brows went up. "That soon? I hoped we could all go out. Well, next time."

My stomach flipped over. "Yes, that would be fun." I eased into a light conversation about the team and flight. I appreciated her distraction, though I couldn't stop my pulse from racing at the start of the game.

My eyes darted from the Jumbotron countdown to the match. Our breakup. My leg was bouncing up and down so hard, Kayla called for someone to bring me a blanket, thinking I was chilly. I took it, though I placed it on the side of my seat and took some deep breaths as I tried to figure out what I was going to do when the game was over. Did Dylan have a plan?

He hadn't set it up well by the way he held me before the match and that was making this even more confusing. Or was I reading too much into it because I had become attached? More than likely, and that was my fault. I didn't know how to hold back my feelings. I had put them all the way out there but lost in the end. Now I had to show that I could handle myself. I'd go and shake his hand and thank him. I wouldn't make a scene. Nicola and Salvatore would tell Raymond I had redeemed myself professionally.

My pep-talk centered me and, though my stomach soured and my heart ached, I cheered and clapped along with Kayla and the other fans in time with the match, celebrating Dylan's goal as well as Tyler's. New York F.C. were playing well. Nonetheless, LA Galaxy recovered in the second half with a penalty score that evened the match to 2-2. It was down to only five minutes left and my heart was beating so hard I could feel it in my ears as I watched the team rush over the field to try to score. Every player they had seemed to stay around Dylan. The ball went from goal keeper to goal keeper, without anyone getting it long enough to score.

"A tied game," Kayla grumped. "They will get them tomorrow."

"I'm sure they will." Bile rose in my throat and I took a quick sip from the complimentary water bottle before stumbling to my feet and down the short flight of concrete stairs that led to the tunnel where the team exited, to meet Dylan.

I congratulated the team as they passed by while I waited. He finally appeared a yard or so in front of me and my heart jumped in my throat. His lean, powerful body moved forward with the magnitude and grace that surrounded him. He was positively a vision, and it was no wonder that all along the path people were vying for his attention. I had it for a while and I had fallen completely in love with it and every moment I had spent with this amazing man.

Even with my inner turmoil, I couldn't look away or just leave, though I needed to. I waved around my trembling arm, and his gorgeous eyes honed in on me. The electricity of our connection flowed as he rushed forward to me. I tried to hold back, but Dylan lifted me up and I put my arms around his damp neck to hug him. I couldn't stop myself from inhaling deeply and relishing his scent, even as sweaty as he was. I put all of my emotions into that hug and couldn't stop the tears that fell down my face when he placed me down on my feet.

His brows knitted, and I knew I must have messed up. "Why are you crying?"

"I'm sorry," I stuttered. "I'm not good with stuff like this."

"It's okay," he soothed and kissed my cheek. "I need to do press—"

I took in a quick breath. "I won't take any more of your time. Thank you for the opportunity. I'll say goodbye here and head to the airport."

Dylan's brows went up like he was surprised. Was it supposed to happen later? I wasn't sure. "What is this? You leaving?"

"Dylan, can you take a picture with us?" A gentleman in a suit holding the hand of a toddler dressed in a jersey came over to where we stood.

"Just one minute," he snipped at the gentleman. He moved me farther away and over to the wall, where he caged me in. "You don't have to go back to New York City until tomorrow night. We are going back to the hotel."

I lowered my head to the top of his chest and closed my eyes. I could do this. "I'm leaving. You and I are, and will always be, friends. Your star will rise and you will continue to shine. I'm proud of you. I love you."

"You...you love me?" he repeated it like a question. "You love me and are leaving me?"

"Yes. I know you don't love me, and I accept it," I stammered. I shook, and he wrapped his arms around me. All I wanted to do was stay, but I couldn't. I moved to get free, but he grabbed my waist.

"You can't say you love me and then walk out of my life. Give me some time to think about it...about us, damn it."

I furrowed my brows. "Why are you acting surprised? You don't need to keep pretending. You don't need to think about anything anymore. I didn't have to think about loving you. Did you feel my love?" I pushed on his chest and sucked in air. "You know what? Never mind. Listen, you ever need me, I'll be there for you, but right now, let me go." My voice broke.

He clasped the sides of my face, his eyes shimmering. "I need you fucking now, Brooke. You need me. Don't do this to me right now. Stay and let's talk."

Now he was pissing me off. He was the one who set this stuff up in the first place.

"What for? Your new contract doesn't allow it," I hissed.

He glared at me. "The new contract was to help the both of us."

I grimaced. He called that *help*? I was so out of here.

I twisted so much he had to let me go to avoid making a scene, and when he did his eyes were blazing. He was about to try to hold on to me again, but I hurried off into the crowd and heard him call behind me.

"What the fuck, Brooke? Wait."

I didn't. I rushed forward and into the crowd, allowing it to close around me. The press and his fans were calling to him and I was sure he would answer. Still, I pushed on until I found a clear path to the exit and got in the line with the fans. I reached in my purse and patted over the tears that were tunneling down my face that I couldn't stop.

I had thought I was clear when I got to the front of the venue, but a paparazzo immediately called out my name and the path to the car was blocked. I had no security or staff around for help. I turned in a tight circle to flashes of cameras.

"Where is Dylan?"

"Is he cheating? Is that why you're crying?"

As if the tears weren't enough, they were pushing for a story too. I was hot and frazzled and ready to scream for them to go away, but I had my image to maintain.

I wiped the tears and tried to smile. "I'm not feeling well. Would you please let me get to my car?" But no one moved. They kept pressing in. I didn't know what to do.

"Brooke."

I turned and my heart sank. It was Tyler instead of Dylan. They had cleared a path for him to reach me. He asked, "Are you okay?"

"I just want to get to the car," I sniveled.

He put his hand on my back and pushed the crowd forward to the door.

"You with Tyler now?"

"No, we are not together," I said and wiped my face.

"What do you think of the rumored Pollini role for Dylan?"

"I wish Dylan the best in his success."

The press surged forward and Tyler had to try a few times to open the door

"No more questions. No comment," Tyler said, struggling at the door. After helping me into the car, the crowd and press started haggling him.

"You can get in," I called and slid across the seat

Tyler got in and closed the door. An explosion of flashes of cameras behind us went off as we rode away from the stadium.

"Why aren't you leaving with Dylan?" he asked.

I burst into tears. His hand came out and touched my

arm, and I jumped. "Don't… Thank you for helping me back there, but I'll be fine."

"I apologize. Are you heading over to the hotel?" Tyler asked.

I wiped my eyes. I didn't want to go back to the hotel and be without Dylan. I wasn't ready to go back to New York City. There was only one other place I could go. "No. Please tell him to take me to the airport. I'm going to Seattle."

CHAPTER
TWENTY

Dylan

The second Brooke ran off, I regretted letting her get away. But with the press cameras going off, sponsors and fans thrusting their kits in my face, I didn't have a clear path to get to her. Not that they would care how destroyed I was. They wanted me to stick to the routine—smile nice and sign. When all I felt like doing was fighting.

What the fuck happened? We tied the game, but I got the role in the Pollini film and that was a good reason to celebrate. Brooke was genuinely happy for me. That I was sure of. But then she told me she loved me, and before I had a chance to think, she broke up with me. Yeah, it was a lot to take in in the middle of everything around me. I've never told a woman I loved her before. But that didn't mean I wouldn't.

Fuck. I cocked up. I needed to get out of this and find her.

The crowd swelled and moved me farther into the stadium where more fans jerked me for attention. I grimaced and scribbled my name, snatched and tossed back absently the items shoved in my face. They were excited, and I was being a rightful bastard, but at the moment I didn't care. This went on until I spotted Knox in front of me. Good on him. He had pushed through the mass to save me.

"Dylan needs to go and meet with the team," he yelled out to the disappointed fans. Truthfully, Lance hadn't called a meeting, but it worked. They parted a path for our exit. I was grateful for the help and told him when we were safely inside the changing rooms.

He grinned. "You needed it."

I went straight to my phone and tried Brooke. The call went straight to voicemail. I was gutted but, not giving up, I sent a text.

Dylan M. Pierce: *We're not done.*

I wasn't done with her. It couldn't be over. Knox eyed me curiously, and I told him Brooke did a runner.

"I thought better of Brooke. She's flaky like her silly friend?" he asked. His tone was harsh.

I pulled off my shirt and smirked. Gemma had become a dirty word since she had left him at the restaurant. I didn't blame him, but Brooke wasn't like that. "Nope, this is different. Brooke...had a good reason. I need to find her."

"You know where she went?" he asked.

"No. Her plane ticket was for tomorrow," I answered. "She was staying in my room." A light bulb went off in my head. She could be at the hotel. I put my sweaty shirt back on and started shoving the rest in my bag to leave.

"You'll only make a fool of yourself, running out there blind," Knox said. "Come back to mine, have a drink and think this shit through before rushing off like a love-crazed idiot."

I furrowed my brows. Love? I felt like shite—my chest burned and my stomach ached. It must be love. Fuck it. I was in love with her, no use denying it. "You're barking. I'm not a crazed idiot."

He had a point. Running around would just look desperate. I needed to figure this shite out. Good on Knox to step in and help me out again. "Thanks…. mate."

He slapped my shoulder and grinned. "Just make me the best man."

"I'm not getting married." I gave him a push as I passed him. But, hell, that idea didn't bother me as much as it should have. I was totally gone on her.

After we both finished and loaded our bags, we left through the security exit for the hotel in one of the private cars reserved for the team. When we arrived, instead of going to Knox's room, I went straight across the hall to mine. None of Brooke's belongings were there. I doubted she had come here at all. She was gone.

Heaving a sigh, I went across the hall to Knox's room. He ordered us a couple of steaks and wine. I wasn't hungry, but I nibbled, and downed most of the wine. That got me talking. I told him about the acting gig and Pollini role. My time with the team would soon be over.

"So you plan to bring Brooke with you to Los Angeles when you move here?" he asked.

"I hadn't planned for it," I replied. Truthfully, I hadn't thought that far ahead with us. The only thing I was certain of was that I didn't want to be without her.

"Doesn't she act or something over in New York? I mean, you hired her for promotions. She can't disappear," he said and finished off his wine.

I rubbed my jaw. That was something that was bothering me about the way she left. I hadn't taken much notice of it, but I sure knew who to call for answers. I took out my phone and called Salvatore. He answered on the first ring.

"You celebrating?" Salvatore asked with a lift to his voice.

"No, I'm not. Brooke left." I got up and moved to the door.

"Well, I'm sure you'll be fine soon," Salvatore replied.

Turning to Knox, I called back. "Going across to mine."

"I don't believe I will be." I closed my door and started to pace. "Not without her. But there was something odd she said before she left. When I asked her to stay and talk, she said the new contract wouldn't allow her to do it."

"Uhm…maybe she was mixed up and jumbled her words," he replied and coughed.

"That doesn't sound like her. I'd like to see the new contract she signed. Can you bring over a copy?"

"I don't believe I have it with me, but I do know she signed it…" He muffled the phone.

"Please ask Nicola for a copy," I said.

"She's with me, but she said the contract was standard." His tone was hesitant. "She agreed to take the money."

"I'd still like to see it now, thanks. I'm in my room." I hung up.

The hairs on the back of my neck stood up. He was acting strangely. Rarely had I ever asked much of him and usually when I did he was quick to help. Did he know something and wasn't telling me?

I paced for a few minutes on what I should do and came up with the idea to call Raymond next, but Salvatore arrived with Nicola. We took a seat at the dining table.

Nicola handed over a manila envelope, and I took out the contract and started looking it over. "Do you think this is necessary? I'm sure by now Brooke has announced the end of your relationship to the press."

I lifted my chin to them to save face, but I felt that weirdness in my chest again. "If she did, they'll wait for a word from me and I will tell them we are still together."

"Why? Your relationship ending now isn't a bad thing. You told me you weren't taking Brooke with you when you move to Los Angeles," Nicola said, her voice strained.

"I wasn't going to, but I've changed my mind," I said. I found a weird amendment I hadn't seen before that read: *"I agree to stop all contact with Dylan M. Pierce at the end of the Los Angeles game."* Brooke's initials were signed next to it. "What the hell is this?"

"We proceeded to offer Brooke money to move on since we all knew you were getting the role in the movie. She readily agreed to the conditions and signed," Salvatore said.

I narrowed my gaze. She didn't want to do it, I had gotten that much out of her. "Who the hell told you that you had the right to make her break up with me?"

"We handled this like you asked us to handle all the other women. It was to keep things under control with the press and your new image," Salvatore said. "It was the whole reason you agreed to this in the first place."

"Originally, but I told you we were seeing each other. You fucking went behind my back and tried to ruin the one good I had going for me." I ripped the contract in half. "Was Raymond in on this shite?"

"He was interested in the best for Brooke. He didn't want her hurt or without compensation," Salvatore said.

"Oh, I'm sure the two of you had him thinking I wanted to do that to her." My chair fell down when I stood up. "I'll have a talk with him, but Brooke wasn't just any woman. She was special…"

"You don't even know her," Nicola snipped.

I glared at her. "Is this all about you? I do know Brooke. She could have milked our relationship, but she didn't. She followed everything I needed her to do. When she got her acting job, she put her all into her performance. She deserved to be there. Even after getting the money, she kept her job at that goofy themed restaurant. When Rocco was sick, she dropped everything and was at our side. Brooke's hardworking, caring and loving." And how could I not love her? How could I let her go? *I can't. She's mine.* "She deserved better than to be treated like shite by people who were supposed to represent me."

"I'm sorry," Salvatore said.

I narrowed my gaze. "Too late. Since you both find

it's too hard to handle a man like me and that you need to go behind my back to ruin my relationship, you're both done representing me. There is no way I'd ever trust either one of you again. You can go now."

"I believe you are making an impassioned mistake, and I apologize," Salvatore said.

"Save it for Brooke," I said. He rose and left the room.

Nicola squared her shoulders. "I'll get one of the other lawyers in the practice to finish your contract with Pollini and then you're free to choose your next counsel."

I gave her a curt nod. "I'll agree to that, but that's it."

We moved to the door, where she paused in the doorway. "I'd like an answer, if you'll indulge me."

I let my hand fall away from the doorknob, and waited.

"You have known me for years, and we were together for months. What made you choose her? I mean, I'm hardworking and never took advantage either. I would have been around for you and your dog if you'd asked me," she said.

"It wasn't just those things I named," I admitted. "Honestly, I believe it was a bunch of little things."

She lowered her head. "Love. You love her."

I didn't answer, but it was clear Nicola had been hiding her feelings. Or more likely, I chose to ignore them. I didn't feel that way about her.

"I'm sorry, Dylan," she said. "Thank you."

I pressed my lips together. "I'm sorry our working friendship had to end this way."

She moved in for a hug and I stepped back and folded my arms.

"Goodbye, Dylan," she said sadly. She hurried down the hallway.

"Goodbye," I muttered.

Knox's door suddenly opened, with him yelling, "Dylan deserves to know. I don't give a shit."

Lance appeared, grabbing his shoulder behind him. "I called him and he will call me back. Don't make him crazy when we don't have the facts."

"Alright?" I asked and pushed open my door, letting Knox stalk past.

"You've got to see this. I can't believe this shit," Knox said. He went straight over and grabbed the remote off the coffee table and turned on the television.

"Dylan, listen to me," Lance said. "We will figure this out."

"Figure what out?" I closed the door and noticed Lance hung back. "What are you two talking about?"

"Just watch." He flipped through the channels and stopped at a celebrity trash gossip show.

"I don't watch that shite," I complained.

"He doesn't want to watch it. Turn it off," Lance yelled.

Knox folded his arms, ignoring him. "No can do, dude. Just wait."

I was about to turn it off myself when Brooke appeared on the screen, crying with Tyler's hand on her back, the stadium as a backdrop.

"Pierbrooke is over. Dylan Pierce and Brooke Sullivan ended their sweet romance. The tumultuous dump at the game and her rebound with Tyler Wilson."

"We are not together," Brooke said and paused. "I wish Dylan the best in his success." The sound was out of sync, but I couldn't deny it was Brooke with Tyler.

"That means the heartthrob heartbreaker Dylan Pierce's hot ass is back on the market. Go get him, ladies."

I knocked over a table. Tyler had had his hands on Brooke and left with her. "I'm going to kill him."

"He deserves it," Knox goaded.

I was charging for the door and was pushing Lance out of the way, when he tackled me to the ground. "Are you serious, Lance? If it was Kayla, you would have lost your mind."

"True, but I'd want the whole story. Now, I called Tyler," he said. "He had a bad connection, but he said he'd phone back. Knox, I came to you for help, not to start shit."

"I am helping," Knox said, giving us a hand to our feet.

I headed back for the door, when Lance's phone buzzed and he looked at the screen. "It's Tyler. Let me talk to him."

"You're dead," I yelled out.

Lance moved away and yelled into the phone. "You with Brooke?" he growled.

I paused, my pulse in my throat and waited for the answer.

"No. He's on his way back to the hotel from dinner," Lance said.

"Tell him he needs to come to Dylan's room," Knox said.

"Good idea. I'll kick his bloody arse when he gets

here," I growled.

"No. You're safe as long as you did nothing. Yeah, I'll stay," Lance told him. "I'll remind Dylan we have a game tomorrow." He hung up. "He said nothing happened, but I told him I'd stay and supervise. You going to listen?"

"I'll see how it goes," was all I said and promised. Lance may as well suspend me. There was nothing Tyler could say that would excuse him for leaving with Brooke. There was no way I was leaving without kicking his arse the first chance I got.

But I bided my time. I sat down and stewed while they watched and chatted about American football to wait. A knock sounded on the door and I was on my feet. So was Lance, and he was quick to block me while Knox answered.

"Are you going to be at the next game?" Lance said.

I crossed my arms. "Probably not."

He blew out his breath. "Damn. Just listen, it might be alright."

Tyler came all the way into the room with a sheepish grin on his face.

I could've kicked all their arses with the amount of adrenaline pumping through me, but I sat back down. I needed to know what happened with Brooke.

"Hey, man. It's just like I told Lance, nothing happened," he said and sat down in a chair. "I saw Brooke running, and she was being hassled by the press. I'm the one who helped her get in her car safely."

"But you put your big arse in there too," I said sarcastically.

Knox found my remark funny. I was serious.

Tyler shrugged. "I was trying to make sure she was okay."

"That wasn't your place," Knox said with snark.

I nodded. Good on him. "Where did you go with her?"

Tyler rolled his neck. "We rode to the airport. I went with her to change her ticket to Seattle. She said something about her parents. I left once she went to the security check, where the press would leave her. She was crying the whole time. I got a call from Lance and called him back after I finished my dinner, and now I'm here."

"That's it?" Knox asked skeptically.

My jaw ticked. I doubted Tyler's story too. He wasn't the comforting kind unless he also got to feel her up. I flexed my fists.

"Yeah. I'm a shit." He chuckled. "But I'm telling the truth. Hell, ask her. She didn't want anything from me."

Lance exhaled loudly. "What do you think, Dylan?"

My lip quirked. I was sure Brooke could take care of herself, but I didn't want her in any situation where she had to.

I stood up with my hand out. "Fair enough."

Tyler reached for it and I saw my chance. Grabbing his hand fast, I pulled him forward and connected my fist to his jaw, then let him go.

He fell over the chair with a thud

Lance and Knox moved between us.

"I said I didn't touch her," Tyler yelled, clutching his jaw. "What the hell, man?"

"That's for touching her, getting in the car, sitting next to her, and fucking breathing the same air as what's mine,"

I snarled. "You ever try that shite again, you won't be able to get up."

"That's fair, Tyler," Knox said, coming to stand next to me. "Brooke wasn't for you to look after. How'd you like it if I went to pick up Zoe?"

Tyler's face contorted. "I don't even want you saying my sister's name."

"I thought so," Knox said and smirked. "If I ever catch you with mine, you'll get more than a sore face."

I scoffed. "You got someone?"

"Nope. Too much living to do, my man," Knox said. "You go get her."

"You're off the next game," Lance said with annoyance to me. "As long as Tyler can still play?"

"I'm fine," Tyler said, still holding his face. "Thanks for getting me to come here and letting him hit me."

"You should be happy we are here. It would have gone worse if he had caught up to you on your own," Knox said.

True enough. But I was done with the Tyler drama.

"I'm heading to Seattle," I said.

"Understood," Lance said. "But we need you back for the rest of the games this week." He helped Tyler up, and they left.

I went to the closet to get my bag.

"You know where to go?" Knox asked.

"I suppose I could ask her friend Gemma," I said and glanced back at Knox.

Knox's smile disappeared. "Alright. You need anything let me know. See you later."

I phoned Gemma.

"I just got off the phone with Brooke. What do you

want?" she said, answering with an attitude.

"I want to see her. Do you have her parents' address?" I asked.

"They live in Redmond, but I wouldn't go there. They don't like you. Her father offered her a good deal. She might be moving back permanently."

"She wants to act, not waste her time there," I said.

"Yes, she does, but without work, and my leaving for tour, she will have a hard time making ends meet," she said.

I cursed. She wouldn't have with the new contract I had for her.

"You know that already," Gemma continued. "I don't want you hurting her. She's a great person and deserves to be with someone who will appreciate her."

"I do," I muttered. I wasn't going to explain myself to her.

"You still mad about the Knox thing? He wasn't serious anyway," she said.

"You'll never know," I said coolly.

"I shouldn't tell you for that snark," she said and blew out into the phone. "I'll warn her you know."

"That's fine," I replied. "Please give it to me."

She gave me the address, then hung up on me. I didn't care. I got what I wanted. I knew where Brooke went and where to find her.

I had my things packed, checked out and I stood by the concierge and waited for the car to the airport. And I was just out the door when a buxom blonde came burrowing up to me. She threw her arms around my neck and tried to give me a kiss that landed on my cheek.

"What the fuck are you doing?" I pulled her off me and wiped my cheek. The flash of cameras alerted me we weren't alone.

"You don't remember me?" she huffed, thoroughly put out.

"No, I don't," I said icily. "If I did you'd know better than to grab me. Now go away."

She threw her bag over her shoulder and stomped back inside the hotel.

The press, however, weren't bothered to capture her retreat. They had all the gossip they wanted and were expecting from someone like me. The old me. The new me wasn't going to tolerate it. I went over to the paparazzi at the end of the taxi ramp.

"My side of the story. She grabbed me and I left. There is my cab." I pointed at the ajar door where the bell person was placing my bag in the trunk. "I'm heading to the airport to see Brooke Sullivan. We are still together. I suppose that's not as interesting a story, but it's the truth."

I didn't stay to answer questions. I got in my cab and left.

Whether they bought my story or not, it wasn't pretend anymore. Brooke belonged with me. And I wasn't leaving Seattle without her.

CHAPTER
TWENTY-ONE

Brooke

I sat on the window seat in my old bedroom at my parents' house in Redmond.

The two-hour flight and forty-minute cab ride had me at their doorstep just as they were sitting down for dinner. My tear-streaked face had them resisting an interrogation at my sudden arrival. We had agreed to discuss it after I had some rest, but I doubted I would be able to. It wasn't just because of the non-disclosure agreement from the contract, but because I wasn't ready to face the truth. I had lost Dylan.

A summer night's rain had just begun to pour down over the lush greenery surrounding the estate. Even with all this beauty, I still longed for my cramped apartment in the East Village and my life there. But now I couldn't imagine it without Dylan. In a short time, he had left his mark on everything in my world, from my jobs, apartment, and even my friends.

He had left his mark on me and on my heart, which was now left broken. I loved every part of that cocky, beautiful, dirty, demanding, caring, playful, sexy man. I didn't know how to get over him, but I had no choice. He didn't love me back.

His surprise and anguish when I told him I was leaving hit me square in my heart. It was as if he didn't know about his contract to be rid of me. Had he regretted it? I didn't know, but what I did know was that he didn't want to be with me, and knowing that was enough to leave and protect my heart. I had to rebuild my life and career without him.

What career? I'd been as good as cut from the cast of *Rent* with the possibility of some stagehand work in the future. Therefore, with just a few sporadic shifts at Colby's for work, I was basically unemployed. As for my apartment, Gemma would be moving on soon with her *Les Misérables* tour, so I wouldn't be able to afford to keep it. The only money I had coming in was the money from my agreement with Dylan. And that was as good as over now that we weren't together. Truly, there was no way I could be around him and not want to be with him. What was I going to do? I wasn't going to be able to fix this tonight.

Swinging my legs back down onto the floor, I almost tripped over the fancy athletic shoes on my feet. It was silly to put them back on after my shower. But that little material of rubber and design had transformed from its original property to a living symbol of the most precious and happiest moments I'd shared with Dylan.

My heart felt heavy as I took them off and placed

them at the end of the bed, then curled up on my side and tried to sleep.

The sound of the doorbell ringing woke me up with a start. It kept on chiming within the space of a few seconds. *What the hell?* Someone was either determined to get inside or one of my parents had locked themselves out. Unlikely, but whatever the cause, I was awake now and would help.

Sitting up, I grabbed my shoes and terrycloth robe before rushing down the stairs to the front door to answer it. When I got to the last step of the staircase, I found the door ajar with my father blocking the entry. He was facing off with someone, in his pajamas and slippers. "Who are you and why are you here?" he yelled. His gray hair suffered from the worst case of bed-head.

"I'm Dylan. I'm here for Brooke."

My heart jumped in my throat. "Dylan?"

He moved forward into the doorway so I could see him fully. His fitted top and jeans were creased and damp from the rain as well as his blond hair that was piled up in one of his man-buns. He still looked incredibly handsome. But what drew me was the strength and determination on his face at seeing me. Was he upset? Had something else happened?

"This is my…" My voice trailed off.

"Her man," Dylan answered cockily.

My face warmed. *My man?* "This is Dylan Pierce, my

ex-boyfriend. He can come inside. I didn't know he was coming."

"Gemma told me she'd phone that I was on my way here," he explained as he stepped inside.

I frowned. My phone must be out of power. I wasn't in my right mind when I arrived here. That didn't explain what he was doing here.

My father slammed the front door. "So that gives you the right to come here in the middle of the night and lay on the doorbell, waking up the whole house?"

"Yes. I wasn't going to waste a minute away from Brooke." His piercing blue gaze shifted away from my father and fell on me, and my heartbeat picked up and thudded against my ribcage. "Brooke, I've come for you."

I parted my lips. I couldn't move from the spot where I stood at the bottom of the stairs. "But the contract…"

"Salvatore and Nicola went behind my back, and I fired them. I wasn't aware of their plan to let you go. I'd never agree to have you away from me."

I touched my chest. "I didn't know."

Mom appeared in her robe and slippers. Her reddish-brown hair was in a braid hanging over her shoulder.

Her green eyes filtered through us all standing there, then settled on me, and asked, "Your boyfriend?"

I tilted my head down. "I don't know."

"Yes," Dylan bellowed and came forward and shook her hand. His nearness caused my insides to tremble with excitement.

"I don't care who you are, but my daughter isn't going anywhere with you," my father said. "She's going to college for business management and will be opening a dance studio here."

"Excuse me, Father, but I haven't agreed to anything," I spoke up.

"She's an actress not a dance instructor," Dylan said. "Have you ever seen your daughter perform? She's brilliant."

"Not that I need to explain this to you, Mr. Pierce, but acting takes more than a performance," Father replied. "It—"

"It takes talent and perseverance," Dylan said, cutting him off. "Your daughter is committed and passionate about her art."

"That leaves her in debt and without money," my father said contrarily.

"Allister," my mom grumbled.

"No, Anna," he said. "Brooke needs stability and not to continue to waste any more of her life on unattainable dreams."

I folded my arms. "I don't feel I have a wasted life. I have gained experience and achieved some success. All of my experience wasn't a waste."

"So why are you back here?" my father griped.

I blinked at him.

"Damn you," Dylan said under his breath. He grabbed me in his arms and hugged me tight. "She can't come back home unless she does what you want her to?"

"I'm alright," I whispered to him, soaking in the comfort of his arms. "I'm used to it."

"Bullocks," he gritted out. "I don't care who you are, don't ever hurt her in my presence."

"I didn't hurt her," my father said tersely. "You can't

come in my home and boss me around."

I eased out of his arms and lifted my chin. "Dylan didn't mean any harm, and I never did tell you both why I had come back home. I came back because I was hurt…"

Dylan ran his hand over my back soothingly.

"I needed to regroup and make a plan. I never said I came here to give up and stay. Raymond said—"

"Your agent, Raymond?" my father interjected, and laughed a little. "He is stringing you along for the money. Listen to reason. Anna, please tell her."

We all turned to her.

"Brooke… Mr. Pierce," she said.

"Please call me Dylan," he said, a soft smile on his lips.

"Dylan." She smiled back at him. "I want my daughter happy and not struggling to support herself. Allister wants the same. You must understand that we are her parents. We aren't trying to hurt her. We love her."

"I love her too," Dylan said.

My heart soared at his profession. "You do?"

He caressed the side of my face. "Yes, I do. I came here to tell you because I wasn't going to wait once I realized I did." I wrapped my arms around him. "I love you."

He rubbed my back. "Salvatore and Nicola were supposed to tell you I wanted to help with your career. In fact, I believe you'd be better off coming with me and Rocco to Los Angeles."

"Rocco?" Mom asked.

"My dog," Dylan said.

I opened my mouth to respond, but my father did it for me.

"We Starlings don't believe in taking handouts," he

said. "Brooke, is that what you want to do? Live off this man? That's the easy road. We raised you better than that."

Dylan tensed in my arms. "Leave it," I pleaded.

"Like hell I am," he said. "I don't give a shite about what you think, Mr. Starling. My helping Brooke is a hand up, not out. Unlike you, I believe in Brooke's ability to succeed at her acting dream. She needs help and she'll get it from me."

My father snorted. "Semantics—"

"Please stop arguing," I interrupted. "I'm not going to take Dylan's money or offer, Dad."

My father sighed in relief.

Dylan snorted. "Fuck this. In less than a day, your father has poisoned you to think accepting help is bad. You'll figure it out with me, but I'll be damned if I leave you here. Get your things right now, Brooke. We are leaving, even if I have to drag you out with only what you're wearing."

"She most certainly will not," my father said heatedly. "This is my house and you will respect me. I let you in out of courtesy, but now you've out-stayed your welcome. Brooke said she doesn't want to go with you. Now leave."

I took Dylan's hand. "Dad, I never said I didn't want to go with him. I said I didn't want to use him to further my career. Going with him to Los Angeles without my own plan wouldn't be something I'd want to do."

"Fine. I'll get Raymond to help build you a team and more connections to further your career," Dylan said.

"Throw more money out the window," my father hissed.

Dylan puffed up his chest. "My money. None of it is

any of your business. You can take your house, but Brooke won't stay in this toxic environment. She will come with me."

"Do you believe this man?" My father was flustered. "She's my daughter. She's not your property."

"She's an independent adult woman whom you and your lovely wife raised well," Dylan said, looking at my mom. From the grin on her face, she ate his compliment up. "I'm not seeking your consent if I can help her. She will learn to take it because that's what people do when they have the means and care about you. They don't make you feel bad when you need help. They give and delight in your success. That's how I was raised and that's how I will treat Brooke. I enjoy watching her when she's happy."

My heart swelled too big for my chest and I pressed myself into Dylan's arms. His speech was pure. I was left without doubt about the love he had in his heart for me.

My father finally went quiet and my mom went and locked the front door.

"It's early in the morning and we should go to bed," my mom said. "A good night's sleep and we can talk about this in the morning. We have spare rooms..."

"Mom..." I grumbled.

Dylan leaned over my ear and whispered, "There is no way I'm keeping my hands off you."

My face burned. "It's their house."

"The guest cottage out back is not being used. You can...uhm, talk there." She touched my father's arm, who stiffened as he stared between the two of us. "Come on, Allister. Let's give her some privacy."

"Brooke, I still want you to think on my offer. It will

lead to long-term success." He reluctantly followed her up the stairs and disappeared down the hall.

The second they were out of sight, Dylan pulled me into his arms and pressed his lips hard against my mouth. His hand impatiently worked around the robe and inside my panties. "Dylan, my parents are…"

My protest was lost against his tongue that he pushed between my lips. His hand squeezed between my thighs and stroked my sex that grew slick with my arousal from his touch. I whimpered and he broke the kiss long enough to get out his threat. "I'm going to fuck you right here—"

"Not here. It's not far…please." I barely got out my plea, stifling a moan into his shirt as he pushed two of his fingers inside me.

"I need you right now, Brooke. I can't wait."

I was so turned on that I groaned when he removed his fingers, but I wasn't gone far enough to have my parents hear or, heaven forbid, see us making love.

My heart sang. *Making love. Dylan loves me.*

I hurriedly took his hand and he followed me around the staircase to the double doors that led to the paved path to the guest cottage.

I got the key from the fake rock and unlocked the door and, having not been inside for a long while, I got a quick glance at the change in décor. It was nautical in design with a mixture of blue and white furnishings and accents. That was all Dylan let me see as his lips roughly covered my mouth again, our lust and desire immediately rekindled. Our hands rushed over each other, grabbing at the fabric covering our bodies.

He tugged my shirt up over my head and I boldly

reached between his legs and stroked over his erection. "I want you inside me."

"Fuck," he said with a groan and pushed into my hand, then lifted me by my buttocks.

Wrapping my legs around his hips, I hugged his shoulders as he carried me as far as the chaise lounge, where we went down on the large cushion together. His weight came down heavily on top of me.

Our breaths were ragged as we broke away enough for him to get off his shirt, revealing his well-formed upper body that my eyes got a glimpse of before he was back on me. He tore my panties, went down on his knees, buried his face between my thighs and licked my pussy. Gone was his usual finesse. He was impatient, licking fast through my folds and suctioning hard on my clit. I squirmed and moaned underneath him. I loved him wild and lost in need for me, but I wanted him inside me. "Dylan, please."

Fuck, it's sexy when you beg for me." There was that cocky assuredness—another thing I loved about the man. He paused only long enough to get his jeans open to shove his cock inside me. The sudden surge was rough. My inner walls stretched tight around his thickness, which had me letting out a soft cry. It was pleasure and pain at the same time. Dylan leaned his head down and sucked on my nipple, sending sparks right down to my core as he pushed in all the way to the hilt.

"Hold on, love," he gritted out.

I gripped his shoulders as he pounded his cock inside me—hard—moving us at a frenzied pace. It was wild and carnal the way he took me. Every deep plunge of his cock aroused me to no end. I met his thrusts by bucking up under him, taking everything he had as he took complete possession of my body.

"Dylan," I said, letting out a soft cry as he reached down between us. He rubbed my clit and my sex tightened. I was a stroke away from climaxing. He grabbed my hair tightly, exposing my neck enough for him to bury his face against it, and sucked my skin, sending me over the edge.

I screamed out his name again as the orgasm crashed over me.

He pulled out and put me on top. "Ride me," he said in a deep, commanding voice.

I was still feeling the aftershocks of my orgasm, and was so wet from my arousal that his cock slid right in. We let out a collective, ecstatic moan. "You look beautiful," he said.

We smiled at each other while I bounced up and down on his erection, setting my own pace, as he cupped my breasts. My hands moved possessively over the defined planes of his chest and abs.

"You're all mine, Dylan. No one but me."

"All yours. It's you and me, love," Dylan replied, reaffirming my words and possession of him. Our gazes locked, and the air crackled between us. We were in perfect sync. His fingers pinched my nipples and I squirmed as the sensations shot right down to my swollen clit. I squirmed, and stirred my hips as I rode him.

Dylan pushed up hard and grunted. He wanted to take me harder, and I was ready for whatever he wanted to do with me. Placing me on my back, he plunged in hard enough to knock the breath out of me. I moaned approvingly. He growled and picked up his rhythm, slamming his cock inside me over and over again.

I squeezed my eyes shut and deliciously submitted to his erotic drive. The sound of our slick flesh moving against each other filled my ears. My mouth gaped with a hoarse call of his name over and over again.

He answered with hard, deep thrusts of his cock at a frenzied pace that feverishly pushed us up to oblivion. It was raw. The sensations exquisite. I never wanted it to end. My inner walls started clenching, and I bit hard into my lip. Another orgasm was so close. He angled his cock to stroke my clit, and I fell apart, tumbling over into the most incredible bliss of my life.

"Look at me," he commanded, his voice sensually strained.

My eyes returned to his just as he came, releasing in spurts inside me.

I pulled his weight down on top of me and wrapped my arms and legs around as much of his body as I could to hold him. Our breaths were as fast as our heartbeats. We were together, bonded.

I kissed the side of his neck. This was my special, loving man. There was no other man for me.

He lifted me up and carried me over to the master bedroom that had a king-sized bed dressed in white linen and pillows. I stretched like a cat. It was comfy too.

"We will make love again right after your punishment," he said.

I laughed as he put me down and I tugged back the linen. "Punishment? For what?"

He had me straddled and my hands pinned over my head before I could even think about moving away. "How many times did I tell you you're mine and I don't want you anywhere near Tyler?"

I met his eyes as they bore into mine and my heart skipped a beat. "And how many times do I have to tell you that I don't want Tyler or anyone else? He helped me in the car and that's it. The press asked me if we were together and I told him we weren't. They asked about your film too and I said I wished you success."

"Yeah. I saw it all on television earlier," he grumped. "I sorted Tyler out."

I scrunched up my face. "You hit him?"

"Yes, he shouldn't have been anywhere near you."

"Now I feel bad. He didn't do anything but help me. The press was aggressive. I panicked. I was miserable," I said and frowned.

"Because of me. I'm sorry for what happened. I fired them and will fire anyone else who tries to get in my personal life with you," he said. "You could have been hurt and I understand that, but I should have been the one protecting you. You're mine." He let go of my arms, cupped my face and met my eyes again. The intensity of his gaze went straight to my heart. "I'm in love."

My heart leaped. "So am I." I leaned up and kissed his lips. "And you came here for me. I'm safe and I'm with you. I love you."

He smiled down at me. "I love you too."

He rolled to his side, facing me, and ran his fingers from my temple down to my lips. "You're coming back to Los Angeles with me tomorrow?"

"I want to, but let me think on a plan," I said.

His eyes shone and my heart constricted. "I can't leave without you." He was exposed. He looked so lost and vulnerable that I wanted to promise him everything. He had dropped everything to come get me. He had even stood up to my father for me. He believed in me. Yet what my father said had me worried. Would I become complacent in a lifestyle I didn't earn and lose the drive for my own success?

The only way I could prepare was to think through a plan to go forward and ease the worry of this incredible man who lovingly claimed me.

"Just give me the night. I'm sure I will, I just want to make sure I have something going on too," I whispered.

He kissed my lips without a word. Pulling me on top of him, I kissed over his heart that was so big and full of love for me.

Dylan looked so peacefully content, I didn't want to wake him up. So I crept out of the bed and went back to the house so as not to disturb him. What I did know was that I didn't want to leave without him. What could I do?

After a shower, I dressed in a blue shirt and skirt. I packed my bag and grabbed my phone, then went in search of my mom for advice. I found her in the kitchen at the breakfast counter with her morning tea and laptop. Their housekeeper had arrived and was making breakfast.

"We weren't sure what Dylan would eat for breakfast,"

my mom said in greeting. I took the seat opposite her and sighed.

"I doubt Dylan—we—will be staying long." I leaned on my elbow. "I don't know what to do."

"What do you want to do?" she asked, and took a sip of her tea.

"I want to be with him," I said.

She nodded. "He must care a great deal for you, showing up in the middle of the night and fighting with your father. He didn't make much of a good impression."

I shrugged. "He speaks his mind, and he loves me… he believes in me."

She smiled. "You love him, but you don't want to disappoint your father."

I quietly nodded.

"You must follow your own heart," she said. "I love having you here and I'd love it if you'd stay longer, but I told your father you weren't ready to let go of your acting career to become a dance teacher."

"I don't want to, and I do see a possibility of success, but it is a business. There is some risk," I replied.

She lifted her shoulders. "Anything worth it takes determination. Your father said that too. You can work like you worked in New York. I have Mary Kay and a party business. Dylan may want to help you and accept what makes you comfortable and works for you, but don't leave a man behind whom you love and who loves you. That's my advice."

I got up and hugged my mom. "That's exactly what I want to do. Thanks."

Taking out my phone from my bag, I noticed it was

dead. "Mom, do you mind?" She shook her head, and I plugged it into her laptop. After a few minutes it pinged a bunch of times. I checked and found text messages from Gemma and Collin, as well as a voicemail from Raymond with more bad news, I suspected. Gemma's was about Dylan, but Collin's message was odd and came with a link.

CollsB495: I thought you should know the truth.

I furrowed my brow and pressed the link. It was a photo of Dylan looking angry, with a bimbo kissing his cheek. "Back at it with a blonde," was the caption. They were standing before his hotel in Los Angeles. He was wearing the clothes he had on when he showed up last night.

It said he walked back in the hotel and spent the night with her. Liars. But that's what I had thought about him before I knew him. That wasn't my Dylan. He came after me. I did another search and found one article about him flying to Seattle while wearing the same clothing. It was entitled, "Missing in Action. Sneaking off for Sullivan." I laughed and copied the link into the message I sent back to Collin.

Brooke S.: Thanks Collin, but Dylan was in bed with me last night at my parents' home in Redmond.

I next played the one from Raymond. His voice sounded frantic.

"Brooke? Why haven't you called me back? What do you think of the role?"

I sent you the script. I've tried you and Dylan. Did you leave for Seattle? You need to get back to Los Angeles right away to meet the Sanctum team if you are interested in the gig. Call me anytime."

My mouth dropped open. "*Sanctum* wants me?"

"What?" my mother asked. I held up my hand and called Raymond. He answered on the first ring.

"Sorry, Raymond, I just got the message."

"*Sanctum*, the vampire TV series, wants you to audition as the head witch of a new coven that comes to Scranton."

"Witch! Wow. Really?" I said enthusiastically.

"Yes. It's either feast or famine in this business. As you know, *Sanctum* is extremely popular. The star they wanted was a real witchy bitch, so they want someone with a squeaky image, friendly, and eager."

"That's me," I said and grinned. "When? I'm actually in Seattle, after the contract thing."

"Yeah, but you know there are people who will do that to you out here. Salvatore told me Dylan is cancelling and resubmitting a new contract for you, but you won't need it if you can make it there. I have a great feeling about this one, but you know as always there are no guarantees. Do you need me to book your flight?"

"Dylan's here too," I said.

"The both of you," Raymond offered.

"Yes!" I exclaimed.

"I thought so. Call me when you land, and read the script and character profile on the plane. Be yourself. You got this," he said, and we hung up.

"Did I hear right, you're auditioning for *Sanctum*? I love that show," my mom said excitedly. "And now I know there is a witch coven…"

"Mom, don't tell anyone about the coven," I whined, and we laughed. "I must go tell Dylan!"

My father walked in just as I rushed out. "Where are you going?"

I called over my shoulder, "To Dylan. Please tell him, Mom."

Running out the door, I rushed over to the cottage and stopped at the doorway where a freshly showered Dylan was standing in a towel. I touched my chest. "Warn a girl."

He chuckled and pulled off the towel.

I touched my hot face. Damn it. "Dylan, stop teasing. I need to tell you something serious. We need to leave for Los Angeles. Raymond has an audition for me for *Sanctum*."

He gave me a confused look.

"Angst-sexy vampire and witch show," I said.

"Great." He grinned broadly, then came over and hugged me. "Of course we can, but I need to know something first…" He gazed into my eyes. "If by some odd turn of fate, they pass on you, will you leave?"

I shook my head. "No, Dylan. I know this industry is hard work and there are no promises. It hurts, but I'll keep trying and working hard at it and us. I'm not ready to give up on either. What I know more than anything is that I love you and want to be with you."

He wrapped me in his arms, and I hugged him back with just as much feeling.

We packed and put our belongings in the car. Just before we were ready to go, my parents came out to see us off. I hugged my mom and then stopped in front of my father, who was now polished and pressed in a business suit.

Taking a deep breath, I said, "I respect your decisions…Dad. I thank you for the loans and all you've done for me. I was scared, but I will stand tall. I may be leaving with Dylan, but not taking from him. We're going to share with each other. I hope one day you…can be proud of me."

"I am, Brooke. I hate seeing you struggle. I just think when you earn it yourself, it's yours—you own it," he said.

Dylan cleared his throat loudly. "Give it another go, Mr. Starling. You can do better."

My father shot him a pointed look, but added, "But I respect your decision. I love you, Brooke." He hugged me. "Good luck on your audition."

"Thank you, Mr. Starling," Dylan said and held out his hand.

My father shook Dylan's hand. "Allister."

"It's 'break a leg,'" Mom said. "I'm proud of you. Call us and let us know how it turns out. Take care of Brooke," she said, hugging Dylan.

"I most certainly will." He stared at me and I went into his arms. "We will take care of each other," I said and meant it with all my heart.

We rode to the airport, and we walked in with his arm around me, making sure every photographer who wanted a shot got to see that we were indeed still a couple. What was to come, we didn't know, but whatever it would be, we would face it together, in love.

EPILOGUE

Brooke

Close to a Year Later

My character was Rayne Blackwood of the Waverly Coven and I was filming a scene entitled "Scranton Cave Disaster" for *Sanctum*'s final episode before we broke for the spring. Martin, the director, and Tig, our props manager, warned me that we had only the resources to shoot this scene once, and they were counting on me to do my best. But they weren't worried. They had all been welcoming since the day I joined, and treated me as part of the family. I was grateful and appreciated every day to be given the one thing every actor longed for: a chance. And as my dad would say, every chance required hard work, and I was up for it. I wouldn't let my director, cast, or crew down.

The wind machines blew in front of me, whipping

my hair across my face as I crawled on my stomach through the fake rubble and wooden fragments to the mark set on the ground for me to stop. When I reached it, I twirled my hand in a circular fashion, my character's signature gesture for casting spells. It also signaled the crew to start the dry ice smoke to fill the set. The director's chair moved lengthwise to the arch that was the entryway, then back to me. The fake boulders fell down from above and the camera moved in tight to me. I slowly raised my hands, ensuring I hadn't blocked the light on my face, to shield myself from the falling debris. I let out a high-pitched scream, and collapsed. That had the hawk they trained fly down and land on top of my arm. I held my breath to keep myself perfectly still while I waited for direction.

"And…. cut!" Martin yelled. "And that's a wrap. Brooke, that was spot on."

Once the hawk moved on, I bounced up on my feet and did my cutesy twirl that looked silly in my torn green and black velvet costume. The director, cast, and crew around laughed with me. From Daisy Dukes to ancient ritual gowns, I'd come a long way.

My first audition had gone great, but they had me on hold for another three weeks before I was told I had the job. All that waiting would have made me a basket case if it hadn't been for Dylan. He kept me well distracted, lavishing me with love and affection. I was truly spoiled.

The season ended on a cliffhanger, and some were speculating about my return, but I wasn't worried. I had already been offered a new contract. Raymond said they were even talking the possibility of a spin-off series, and

I was readily willing to take it. However, with my new management team and success, I had more bargaining leverage. I also had a few movie scripts coming in, like Dylan, who had been away for the past month finishing up his new film. It was set to begin filming in a few weeks in the city where we met and fell in love, New York.

I missed New York, especially Gemma. She had moved on to a leading role in the Broadway smash hit, *Whimsy*. She and Baloo were still on and off together. I was happy for her. She promised to give us tickets. As for Dylan, he couldn't wait to go and see his old New York City Football Club teammates, especially his friend Knox, who came to L.A. occasionally. He told Dylan that he and the team were doing great, but from the times they were playing in Los Angeles and we got together with them, it was evident they missed him.

I missed Dylan. We planned to take Rocco with us for a getaway in Palm Springs. Although, we could have spent more time in our home in Malibu. It took some getting used to after my small apartment in the East Village, but the ocean view won in the end. Dylan had the weather he craved since leaving England, there was room enough for our families to visit, and it was far enough away from the city for quiet nights together when we both weren't working.

Dylan's role in the Pollini film had become a critic and box office success. They were already talking Golden Globe, Academy, and BAFTA, for best actor in an original film. His first role! He took his parents, along with me, to the ceremony for this year where he was asked to present. His parents both cried. They absolutely adored their son. I had become a darling too. His mom was still hoping for a wedding. I'd take just being with him right now. He was due any minute and planned to pick me up from the set, and that reminded me that I needed to hurry and change. Truly, he was the love of my life. I missed every moment I didn't have with him.

Hugging my costars and crew took up some time, but I made it back to my trailer. I went inside and noticed the dog-sitter hadn't brought Rocco back. He had a walk-on role here too and an Instagram with no less than three million followers. He was famous. We were all famous and the three of us had often been followed by the press. They were waiting for one of us to do something. They had us fighting, breaking up and cheating—all false. We were secure in knowing we were devoted to each other.

I showered and changed, putting back on the striped shirt and jeans I'd worn at three a.m. when I had arrived on set. I smiled as I traced over the sign on the door that had a star and my name. It was crazy. I was a working actress! I was living my dream.

I finished off my outfit with a new pair of crazy-laced athletic shoes from Dylan, and a pang went through my chest. I missed him so much. Though we often called and did video chats, I couldn't wait to be with him. I took out my phone to call, but I heard Rocco's barking outside my trailer. I went to get him, stopping only to take out his special treat for being good. I was so happy to have him with me.

Opening up the door had my heart jumping in my throat. Dylan was standing on the other side, grinning. He had his hair up in a man-bun and had stubble on his chin. His pale blue eyes were tired, but I could also see he was happy to see me. "There is my beautiful Brooke. Miss me, love?"

I smiled broadly. "Did I ever!"

A spurt of adrenaline rushed through my system at having him here, and it had me almost tripping down the stairs. I didn't want to look away from him, not because he looked stunning in his beige linen, tailored pants or the powerful magnetism that surrounded him, but because not one part of me wanted to miss a minute of his company. I was totally smitten.

When I was on the ground, he cupped my face first and kissed over it before kissing my lips. The cast and crew nearby exploded into cheers and claps.

My cheeks warmed, and Dylan ran his fingers over them. "Some things I hope will never change."

"Some? What would you like to change, Mr. Pierce?" I joked.

He answered with another kiss, this one passionate, as his tongue tangled with mine. This kiss had me heating up quickly and our hands moved all over each other. That earned us catcalls.

Rocco barked, wanting in on our love-fest. Dylan reluctantly let me go and we bent down to pet and hug him. He gave Dylan some extra licks and jumps, messing his suit, but he didn't care. He gave me more kisses too. We had all missed each other. "Did you go straight to pick up Rocco?"

"Yes, I did. What do you think of his new collar?" he asked. His tone was light, but his eyes were shimmering.

I eyed him curiously, though I dragged my gaze

away from him and went down on my knee to examine it. Rocco had a small, pink, sparkly box hanging from a string. The air left my lungs and my fingers trembled to remove it. "Is this what I think it is?" My eyes shot to Dylan, and his eyes bore into mine. I shivered.

He held out his right hand. "Stand up, I want to do this properly."

My knees wobbled as I rose to my feet. "You want to do this here? Look at me, I'm wrinkled."

"You're Brooke, the woman I love, and there is nothing else more fitting," he said. He untied the box and the surrounding people took a couple of steps in, though pretending to allow us privacy.

My eyes watered as I watched him take out the ring. It was like my mother's, a French set halo band engagement ring.

He went to his knees. "From the second I saw you at that silly restaurant, I knew I wanted you in my bed."

I laughed. "And you got me there."

"Yeah, I did, but what I quickly found out was there wasn't a time I didn't want to be with you. You're precious and special. I want you to be mine forever. Will you marry me?"

Tears poured down my face. "Yes. I love you."

He steadied my hand and put the ring on my finger. And the cast and crew exploded into rowdy cheers.

A few camera flashes went off, but I didn't care. I was happy someone had captured the best moment of my life. Dylan stood, and we gave a wave to the crowd before kissing again. He was more than I'd ever imagined. We were truly happy together.

Who would have known? What had once been pretend had become our best reality. It was for us. We had our ever after.

The end

Author's note:

The story MATCH-FIT takes place in 2016. The musical *Rent* closed on Broadway in 2008. I intentionally included this show for this fiction because I absolutely love it. I believe it captures the many beautiful and complicated life experiences from a city I love, New York City.

Thank you readers!
If you enjoyed the MATCH-FIT, please review.
I'd love to hear from you.
You can reach me by
FACEBOOK: AMELIE S. DUNCAN'S FACEBOOK
www.facebook.com/AmelieSDuncan

TWITTER: @AMELIESDUNCAN

Visit Amélie S. Duncan's official website

at WWW.AMELIESDUNCAN.COM

Subscribe to Amélie S. Duncan's Mailing List
To be the first to receive updates on new releases and giveaways,
please sign up to be on her personal mailing list.
SUBSCRIBE NOW
http://eepurl.com/baQzb5

ACKNOWLEDGMENTS

Thank you to my dear husband and best friend Alan. I love you.

Thank you to wonderful group of people that helped me with Match Fit. I greatly appreciate all your help and hard work.

Thank you to, Silvia Curry, Deanna, Hermione B., Mia Sage, and Betty for their beta critiques.

Thank you to Lorelei Logsdon for copy editing.

Thank you to Vanessa Bridges, Jessica Kempler, and Laura Marrero for the final proofreading.

Thank you to Sommer Stein of Perfect Pear Creative for the cover design.

Thank you to Champagne Formats for the interior design.

Thank you to the sexy and steamy street team, bloggers, and reviewers.

Thank you readers for reading this story. I most sincerely hope you enjoyed it.

ABOUT THE AUTHOR

Amélie S. Duncan writes contemporary, erotic romances with a dark edge. Her inspiration comes from many sources including her life experiences and travels. She lives on the West Coast of the United States with her husband.

ALSO BY AMÉLIE S. DUNCAN

Match Made (Love and Play Series),
Bad Boys and Show Girls

The Tiger Lily: An Alpha Billionaire Romance Trilogy

The Piper Dreams: A New Adult Romance Trilogy

Little Wolf: A Dark Erotic Standalone

CPSIA information can be obtained
at www.ICGtesting.com
Printed in the USA
LVOW10s1605180717
541773LV00012B/599/P